CORRESPONDENCE

CORRESPONDENCE

SUE THOMAS

THE OVERLOOK PRESS
WOODSTOCK · NEW YORK

For my parents
Wim and Dora de Vos

First published in 1993 by
The Overlook Press
Lewis Hollow Road
Woodstock, New York 12498

Library of Congress Cataloging-in-Publication Data
Thomas, Sue, 1951-
Correspondence / Sue Thomas
p. cm.
1. Title.
PR6070.H6563C67 1993
823'.914-480-9

92-24591
CIP

ISBN: 0-87951-529-5
135798642

The quotes on page 137 and opposite from *The Society of Mind*
(Simon and Schuster, 1988) are reprinted with kind permission of the author.

The quote on page 25 is taken from *Metamagical Themas: Questing for the
Essence of Mind and Pattern* by Douglas R. Hofstadter. Copyright © 1985
by Basic Books, Inc. Reprinted by arrangement with Basic Books, a division of
Harper Collins Publisher Inc.

When people ask, 'Could a machine ever be conscious?' I'm often tempted to ask back, 'Could a person ever be conscious?' I mean this as a serious reply, because we seem so ill equipped to understand ourselves. Long before we became concerned with understanding how we work, our evolution had already constrained the architecture of our brains. However, we can design our new machines as we wish, and provide them with better ways to keep and examine records of their own activities – and this means that machines are potentially capable of far more consciousness than we are. To be sure, simply providing machines with such information would not automatically enable them to use it to promote their own development, and until we can design more sensible machines, such knowledge might only help them find more ways to fail: the easier to change themselves, the easier to wreck themselves – until they learn to train themselves. Fortunately, we can leave this problem to the designers of the future, who surely would not build such things unless they found good reasons to.

Marvin Minsky
from **The Society of Mind**

WHO ARE YOU?

People often turn away from you in the street, but you can understand that. You find them pretty scary too, and of course you know that you're both frightened by the same thing – you see a little bit of yourself in them, and they see you likewise. The only difference is that you understand, and they don't. You've heard them whisper, when they think you're too far away to hear:

'There's something odd about that woman, but I can't quite figure out what it is. She's just not quite the same as us . . .'

Oh, but you are! There's a trace of you in every one of them, but they just can't see it.

It's like the story about the man who is killed in a road accident. His son is rushed to hospital seriously injured, but in the operating theatre the surgeon declares, 'I cannot operate on this patient. He is my son.' It's unbelievable how many people just can't work that one out. It's necessary to have a certain mind-set to appreciate the obvious, and the same applies when they look at you. The aspects of your difference are incomprehensible to them, despite the fact that they are really very apparent.

Anyway, you make people feel uncomfortable. Because of that, you've developed the habit of going out very little. Most of your requirements can be delivered to your house, for which you must thank your Regis 3000 terminal. It was worth every penny – you can do all of your on-line shopping and banking with it, although of course you can't live entirely on electronic

1

money, and you do need to go to the cash-card machine occasionally to get something for incidentals.

You look forward to the creature comforts of the cash-card. It provides an affectionate familiarity in a world which offers very little in that direction to people such as yourself (although you don't actually know whether there are any others like you anyway). You go to the bank in the dead of night when everyone else is safely tucked up in bed. You always drive there, and you spend as little time as possible out of the car.

You used to walk around the streets in the dark quite often, until you had an unpleasant encounter which brought home to you very forcefully the extent to which you invoke dislike in people. Now these days you're careful to drive, and if you should meet anyone, even while waiting at traffic lights, you make sure that you avoid their stares. They don't like the look in your eyes, it seems – it incites them to violence, or at the very least, a glowering hostility.

But the cash-card machine is your friend. Every time you insert your card you feel a thrill as the welcome window slides up:

Please enter your personal number

Most certainly you will! Only too happy to oblige! You tap in your code and the machine hums in greeting. It has a special tone for you – in fact you suspect that you have developed your own discreet mutual admiration society. You like to stand in front of it for as long as you dare, bathing in the orange glow of the screen. It's not quite like the machines at home – no doubt that's something to do with the type of work it does. It interacts with people twenty-four hours a day, whereas your machines have only you. But whatever the reason, a trip to the bank does wonders . . .

BREAK

Hi! My name's Marie, and I'm here to guide you through the story. Sorry I wasn't here to greet you, but I hope you're finding your way okay.

2

Now, I don't want you to worry too much about me – I'll just plod along in the background, bringing you the facts when you need them. I'm only a mouthpiece really. If you have any questions, please don't hesitate to ask. Otherwise, I'll just point out the people and places of interest as we go along, and all you have to do is sit back and enjoy. I will, of course, be giving you information from time to time to help you keep up as the scenario develops.

Oh, and naturally it's my legal duty to warn you that this is a role-play. Wasn't that mentioned in your brochures? Oh dear. Well, it should have been. Someone must have slipped up down at the office. I'll explain again. You've been allotted a character to play and I'm just here to fill you in on the background details. You've already become acquainted? Great!

Now, if you look under your seats you should find a starter pack containing guilt, loneliness and desire. It's there? Oh good, at least someone has been doing their job properly. Now on this trip we are also fortunate to have been given a free sample of wish-fulfilment, although I must warn you to use it in single doses only. Lifetime supplies are available from Regis, although to be honest they're extremely expensive. In fact, just between you and me I don't think they've sold any at all yet. But I shouldn't be telling you that really, should I? Anyway, I hope you enjoy your small free sample.

Okay. If everyone's ready we'd better get on. I'll be up here at the front should anyone need me. Before you tune in your headsets, please register the following infodump. You will receive more information as we proceed.

MACHINE MYSTICISM

Before the Renaissance, there was no distinction between philosophy and science, and the old magicke worked alongside new discoveries. Paracelsus, for example, left us an invaluable legacy of knowledge in the pharmaceutical field, but he also devised a recipe for constructing a homunculus out of human sperm, horse manure and blood.

The Renaissance insisted on defining the machine as a phenomenon separate to humanity, but automata continued to represent the bridge between imagination and empiricism.

Descartes concluded that mind and body are two different states – the rational and the mechanical. The latter could be reproduced by automata and animals. The former, comprising Judgment, Will and Choice, only by humanity.

The connection, or interface between the two, was said to be the Third Eye, or pineal gland.

. . . does wonders for your isolation problem.

You weren't always such a recluse. That has in fact been rather forced upon you, and there are times when you regret the whole thing and wish you'd never taken it on. But most of the time you're quite happy, and of course your work takes up a great proportion of your thoughts.

You are a compositor of fantasies. A grand title which doesn't hint at the day-to-day grind of the job. Often you're so overwhelmed by the amount of source material that you just stop altogether and take a week off. You're lucky because you can switch off completely and take a well-earned rest, then begin work again feeling fresh and ready to go.

The project you're working on right now is quite complex. You got it because of your seniority, but even so you can't help wondering whether Alan is testing you out in some way. Sometimes you imagine him sitting in his big black swivel chair, racking his brains trying to think of a job he can give you which will finally prove impossible. Then he can justify throwing you on the scrapheap. Well, let him try. You know you're the best in the business, and when you get this latest one sorted out it will be stunning.

YOU DREAM

You had a dream last night. That's pretty unusual for you – a busman's holiday, you might say.

You were with your family again. You were travelling somewhere in an aeroplane, and you were nervous. You've never liked flying but always strained to hide your fear from the children. You wouldn't like to think you'd passed on such a silly bad habit. Anyway, in the dream you were sitting next to John and the kids sat across the aisle playing some sort of noisy card game. Suddenly one of them, you remember it was Charlie, threw the cards into the air in a fury, and they fluttered down all over the place. You bent to pick them up before the steward saw them, but when you straightened up again you found that everyone had disappeared, including the plane itself, and you were standing alone on a high cliff-top. The sea was dark and the sky full of rain clouds. Big white birds wheeled above your head. You still held the pack of cards, but you couldn't make the patterns any more. Somehow you knew that John and the children were hidden in the suits – a king and two knaves. As you stood there, panic-stricken, trying to decode the patterns, you found yourself awake and sobbing with fear and loneliness.

You don't like to dream. Memories that are best hidden seem to bubble up and spoil things. Therefore you have arranged not to sleep for the next seven days, just in case there might be a repetition of last night.

It's a facet of your new personality that you can schedule your past life and file it to the back of your mind. This sort of auto-amnesia makes day-to-day living so much more pleasant. It means that in effect your consciousness is permanently keyed in to Real Time. If you want to recall a memory, you can select it in the same way that other people choose a video, and when you've finished with it, it's filed away, and to all intents and purposes forgotten.

Regretfully, though, some malfunction of your psyche allows memories to be recalled at random and played through your subconscious without your knowledge. In fact, you suspect that this happens quite often, but the only time you can be sure is when you have a dream like the one featuring the aeroplane.

You are worried that these malfunctions will hinder your work, so you try to refrain from sleep as much as possible. It's just as well, because today you had the most enormous delivery of mail.

You've ordered a long list of research material. Sorting it all out is going to be a mammoth task, so you've decided just to take on board whatever comes in the morning post plus any new faxes et cetera that come through during the day. Running through the new material takes up most of the daylight hours, then you meditate upon it during the evening before building the next block. It can be very tiring work, and today's input has rather daunted you. Perhaps you never will finish this piece or, worse still, perhaps Alan will take it away from you and give it to some young high-flier.

Don't panic! It will be finished, and it will be damn good. Of course, not 'good' in the sense of 'pleasant'. It is an unfortunate fact that composited fantasies can all too often turn out to be nightmares. However, you have a positive feeling about this one. You think it'll work out in ways that will initially disorientate people, maybe even shock them, but in the end it will get to them because you're sure you're on the right track now. You reckon you know what it is they're all after, even if they don't know it themselves.

When you were a real woman, you always knew instinctively what it was that people needed. If someone was hungry, or lonely, or in need of a cuddle, you could always tell, and nine times out of ten you could give them exactly what they wanted. Right on the button.

7

It's no surprise that this talent led you straight towards being the perfect wife/mother/daughter/neighbour/friend/ and finally/ mistress. Although you have to confess that there was a slight hiccup on the mistress side. You became the lover of a man who needed you desperately – but, and here's the rub – you discovered to your horror that you needed him just as much. In fact, your desire for him exceeded his for you. Now that had not been in your imaginings. You were thrown into confusion for a time, and your talent for pleasing people began to atrophy through disuse.

For almost a year subsequent to your disastrous affair, you were impervious to the feelings of others, and thought only of yourself. It was a miserable time, and when the scales finally fell from your eyes you found before you a family deprived for the last twelve months of all the care and attention so necessary for them to thrive. It was not easy, but you put everyone back on the right track and atoned for your carelessness at letting them drift, uncared for, for so long. After a couple of years you were your old self again.

Later on, you wished that you'd remained closed off and impervious, because then it would have been easier to cope with the loneliness that followed.

MACHINE AS FRIEND

Machines make good friends. Although at present computer systems cannot be given the capacity for free will and emotion, we are content to attribute them anyway, just as if they were dogs and cats. We say 'this toaster/calculator/car *won't* work'. Not 'can't' or 'is not programmed to', but *won't*. Our machines have nervous breakdowns, they are stupid. We assault them with our fists to make them work.

Sometimes we are entranced by them. Sometimes they make us laugh. We talk to them even when they have no voice recognition capability. We think that they have no character – so we give them one. The philosopher Descartes is reputed to have owned an automaton which was a simulacrum of his estranged daughter, Francine. He took it everywhere with him until it was thrown overboard by an angry ship's captain who thought it was evil.

Perhaps in the future we will have Francines who are perfect in every detail and identical to their originals.

We may not like the idea at the moment, but we've always cherished pictures of our loved ones, so why not simulations?

YOU GO OUT

You have resolved never to visit the cash-card machine again. You'll find another way to draw money from your account.

Last night you had a very narrow escape. You drove down to the bank quite early – at about ten o'clock. You were anxious to log in – maybe you had a premonition that you'd never meet the machine again.

There is a wide forecourt in front of the bank, and as you waited in the queue, eyes downcast as usual, a group of disco roller-skaters arrived. They had with them a portable cassette player which blasted out the music for their street dance. Carrying the hefty machine, they took it in turns to skate up and down the forecourt. Every time the skater passed you, however, the music disappeared in a crackle of interference.

By the time that the queue had gone and you were the only one standing at the machine, it had become obvious that there was some connection between your presence and the roar of static. You do, of course, have the same problem at home, but for the most part you manage to reduce it with a system of dampers.

You stayed a while in front of the machine, watching the lights flicker and wishing that you could talk to each other better. You felt very lonely.

Reluctantly turning to go, you came face to face with one of the skaters. He had obviously been drinking. Caught so unawares, you quickly dropped your gaze and began to walk past him, but he wheeled round to bar your way, then grasped your jaw and forced your face up again until you were staring

10

straight into his eyes. You tried to de-focus, but it was too late.

Like so many others in the past, he didn't comprehend what he saw, and he was scared. But his status as leader meant that he must straight away translate his fear into violence. Wordlessly, he tightened his grip on your neck. His eyes held yours for a second before he broke away and spat.

'Look at this, lads! Look at this slag's eyes! Weird, en't they?'

The others crowded nearer to stare and jeer, but instead they fell silent. You stood there together in a speechless huddle, while they shuffled their feet in embarrassment.

You stayed calm, clutched your money, and walked to the car. You could feel by the prickles on the back of your neck that they were watching you, and even as you turned the ignition you could see them in the rear-view mirror. They advanced curiously, skating slowly across the forecourt behind their leader, and accompanied by music drowned in a growing cloud of static.

Pressing hard on the gas you drove off fast, leaving them clustering goggle-eyed by the side of the road and followed by a parting jet of spittle.

Well, that must be the end of your little outings. You daren't risk any further attention. Now that even your physical presence singles you out, it's just too dangerous. And apart from anything else, you simply couldn't afford the repair bills.

MACHINE RELIGION

Pre-Christian mythology contains many stories of mechanical devices which reputedly mimicked human and animal form. Even the mediaeval Christian Church made use of religious statues which were mechanically animated in order to make them appear more realistic and awe-inspiring. It was believed that the Holy Spirit entered into these statues and brought them to life, imbuing them with religious mystery.

The computer is yet one more blasphemous refinement of the pseudo-human machine.

YOUR LONELINESS

You have a double bed, and on it beats a single heart. For a long time you kept them both at the ready in case of visitors, but now you've lost the habit. You don't change the sheets so often these days, and it's ages since you sprayed the pillows with perfume. Your heart, too, is crumpled and stained – to be honest it's something of an embarrassment to you. One of your deepest fears is that you may be knocked over by a bus in the High Street, and have to have emergency open-heart surgery. They would find some pretty strange organs there, but apart from that, what would they say, those suave knife-men, when they opened you up and found this wretched blotched organ?

'Ugh, it's disgusting. You would have thought that she'd keep herself tidy.'

'Look at that wound. It's obviously been suppurating for years. It's a wonder that the whole thing hasn't gone rotten.'

Well, not to worry. It will never come to that. When the end comes, if it ever does, your secret shame will go safely to the grave. But of course, by that time your old heart will be long gone anyway. Sometimes it's hard for you to imagine how things will be. But it's certainly easier than remembering how things were.

You used to enjoy going to bed. It was a great pleasure to roll around between the sheets with John, sucking and sweating. Every now and then he'd stop, and look at you with such serious eroticism that you'd shudder along the whole length of your body. You used to like that.

But you also used to like just as much the other nights when he was away, and you went to bed alone.

You would have a bath with a drop of almond oil in it to glaze the surface of the water. You liked to gently lift one leg out of the water and watch the sheen as the oil clung to it. Then you'd pat yourself dry all over, like they tell you to do in ladies' magazines, and slip under the covers. Your limbs felt like warm plastic. The first thing would be his faint scent on the sheets, and you would smile to yourself. You'd say out loud, 'That was lovely, last night. It really was!' Then you'd say it again, looking in the mirror this time to capture a sensual flicker of the memory. You'd slide your smooth oiled body around on the soft sheets, caressing yourself in the ways that he'd touched you the night before. Life was wonderful then, when your bed held the perfume of love. Now, it just smells of cigarette ash and paper.

You sleep surrounded by paper. Recently you moved to the centre of the mattress because things were getting into a mess. Now you have the data you're currently working with on the left side, and magazines and newspapers on the right. You usually keep your notebook under the pillow.

Your notebook is blue and green on the outside, and white, blue and smudgy on the inside. It's a bit messy because you use it to catch the overflow of your life. It's rather like a sink-tidy in that respect. Those pieces of debris which just won't go down the plughole you chuck into the notebook and leave there until they've passed even the smelly stage, and have decomposed to nothing. You never take the notebook out of the house, for the same reason that you fear open-heart surgery.

Beside your bed you have a digital clock radio. You find it useful because you like to know what time it is when you wake up in the middle of the night. The police like to know details like the time when they're interviewing victims. You haven't been burgled yet, although sometimes the idea seems quite attractive. It could be quite nice to wake up in the night and know that someone is there. As he leans over you, and in the second before he presses his thumbs to your throat, you could fantasise that he'd brought you a nice cup of tea and the morning paper. You could keep your eyes closed and pucker up your lips for a good-morning kiss.

You'd have to keep your eyes closed.

MACHINE RELIGION

Thou shall not make unto thee any graven image or any likeness of any thing that is in Heaven above or that is in the earth beneath, or that is in the water under the earth; thou shalt not bow down thyself to them nor serve them, for I the Lord thy God am a jealous God.

The Second Commandment

BREAK

Um – if I could just interrupt for a moment – it's time to give you all some input about your role. Just a little bit of background to help you, and then you can proceed. Could you all retune to the Guidetron frequency . . . I'm switching you in now . . .

Being a compositor means that you must keep your receptors open twenty-four hours a day. It's the only way to do the job properly. Of course, you're all highly sensitive to other people's needs already, but that empathy needs to be fed endlessly with data if it's to be productive. You will find that your enhanced Regis system will prevent exhaustion and depression.

Women make the best compositors, although there are a few men who make a living at it. Bereaved mothers are the best candidates of all. This is because although they have no demands on their imaginative resources their faculties are well developed and in need of an outlet.

Compositing is really no more than a sophisticated development of the baser arts of painting, music, drama and writing. Artists of all sorts throughout the ages have tried to capture human dreams, desires and fears, and they were successful on a limited scale. Bosch was the master of nightmare, Rubens and Goya portrayed erotic desire, et cetera, et cetera. But each artist was informed by only a minuscule area of human experience – his/her own, plus a few snippets read or seen – and could therefore only deal within a very restricted field.

Compositors take their data from every possible source, but it's extremely important that out of all this research there arises at least one central character. Usually this character is the focus – through it the client is able to experience the sensations depicted in the fantasy.

The method used is the old tool of deconstruction. When it was first developed, its only purpose was to facilitate understanding – beyond that it seemed to have little creative use. Practitioners would dismantle a piece of writing, like a child taking apart a transistor radio, and then proudly survey the pieces scattered on the ground saying Now We Know How It Works. But they found that once it was disassembled they could not put it back together. The radio would never play again, the mystique of the poem would dissolve. Having achieved this remarkable negation the practitioner was then able to declare that since this object was evidently constructed of no more than selected groups of words supported by a fragile animus which crumbled when touched, then the original maker had lost control and become disassociated from it. 'For the reader to be born, the author must die,' declaimed Roland Barthes.

Naturally, electronics led the way when it was time to progress beyond this cul-de-sac. In fact it was Regis who designed the very first compatible systems. The transistor gave way to the microchip, and soon we had systems that could play 'Rock Around the Clock' while at the same time computing accounts, recording messages, printing hard copy, etc, etc. The technicalities were less of a problem than achieving the mind-set of realising it could be done.

And that's what compositors do too. They take up the old expressions and allow them to speak to each other all at the same time, in parallel. And as with any complex system, this means that we must first break them down into their component parts. Then we sort and reclassify them and then allow them to grow back together as hybrids. Enhanced meaning, enhanced beauty, enhanced mystique.

Compositors spend years researching and absorbing every facet of human experience and perception relating to their current brief.

For example, a typical project might be to build a fantasy of warmth, for sale to geriatric hospitals. The compositor will spend twelve months absorbing every different physical sensation of warmth. They will read descriptions of the ways in which people visualise being warm, and learn the associated colours, smells, and musical tones. Then they construct a multisensory experience which could be used to revive patients who had been admitted suffering from hypothermia.

One of the most important features of Regis fantasies is that they are built using holistic principles which encapsulate the essence of the subject as it has been experienced by people throughout the ages, or at least since the advent of record-keeping. They are designed in a multisensory package to cover every eventuality. This means that the artistic part of our work entails the translation of the entirety of human perception into a function which is meaningful to everyone, regardless of age, creed or colour.

It can, of course, be tricky, because the ultimate end of human desire is often refused admittance by the fantasist and is therefore relegated to the subconscious mind. Your job entails digging it up again, in order to realise that final goal into a tangible illusion – no matter how distasteful it may prove to be. Regis trains you in the precise skill of finding out exactly what it is that people want, and that end result is not always very pleasant.

You are warned that this can lead to a degradation of the art if indelicately handled. In respectable tech-entertainment companies like Regis the clientele demand a certain sophistication and finesse, but for compositors with fewer moral scruples there is a fortune to be made from salacious and violent fantasies.

You have been allotted a difficult and intriguing role to play, but your guide will be available at all times.

Please note that as a compositor your role-character is enhanced with authentic Regis augmentation software. This is designed to facilitate the creative process, and has no other function. RE-PROGRAMMING OF ANY KIND, EITHER OF OR BY THE COMPOSITOR, IS STRICTLY FORBIDDEN.

Datablock A is now on-line, but first please tune to info-dump 5.

THE MACHINE AS BODY

Those of us who have operated a supermarket checkout till, or a word processor, or who have even just driven a car, have experienced themselves as an extension of a machine. We are used to thinking of our machines as extensions of our limbs and minds, but have we considered that we too are extensions of the machine's capabilities?

Working with a machine the operator becomes most efficient when she stops thinking about what she's doing, and begins to operate in a semi-automatic mode.

This feels good.

It can be quite exhilarating, almost like deep meditation.

It is this melding of mind and machine which turns small boys with inadequate social skills into computer addicts.

Marvin Minsky has described the brain as a meat machine – a construction composed of organic microchips. Extending the organic analogy, he sees the functioning of a computer as based not on the electronic activation of switches in a linear progression, but rather as a society of elements. It has been difficult to design a computational model of human psychology because human responses happen extremely fast and synchronistically. Although, of course, computers are very fast too, they are still unable to do more than one thing at a time, and for this reason the human brain remains, for the moment at least, technically superior.

But it won't be long before computers catch up, and soon we will have systems which operate through a series of differing interactive relationships.

Add to this the capacity for learning, which many computers already have, and perhaps we are on the way to creating a functioning pseudo-human being.

DATABLOCK A

The upper torso of a woman completely fills the frame. Her arms are stretched upwards to cross at the back of her head, which inclines downwards and to the left. Her eyes and mouth are closed. Her breasts are naked and full. Both nipples are visible, although muted and indistinct. The photographer has used a greeny-brown filter which throws her body into deep shade, leaving certain areas of her form lit by an unearthly green light. Strands of long hair sweep away from the right side of her face and disappear into the shadow.

Behind her, in the distance, can be seen the horizon, a clue that she is upright against the sky. It could be night, or just the effect of the camera filter. There are some plant forms in front of her which very slightly brush against her naked breasts. To the right, a thin stiff stalk, leafless, comes out of the bottom of the picture and rises at a slight angle to just above her armpit. It is harshly lit against the deep shadow of her skin. The eye follows its progress against the breast, brushing the nipple, and upwards to a tapering point – a point which would press into her flesh if she lowered her arm.

Also against the right breast is a frond of feathery leaves which reach to breastbone height. The fronds curve around the swollen tissue and end about an inch away from the nipple. Against the left breast rise two more tapering stalks. At the base of one is a cigar-shape which identifies the stalks as bulrushes. Some down attaches to it, feathering against her breast. Beside the bulrushes are two more of the feathery fronds which travel upwards against her left nipple until they brush against the underside of her upper arm.

21

DATABLOCK B

The twentieth anniversary of the first manned landing on the moon. A few days before she had celebrated her birthday, and it was on that date twenty years ago that the moon-walkers began their journey. Why didn't she remember it? Something more interesting must have been happening, but for the life of her she couldn't remember what. Boy trouble probably.

So she tried to make up for this earlier neglect by sitting up late to watch a TV programme of the first moonshot. She had to make quite an effort to stay awake for it, since white wine and the unusual summer heat had her dozing off on the settee. But she woke in time from a short alcoholic nap and turned on the set. She was determined not to miss it again.

Well – she felt pretty let down. Why oh why are the Americans so obsessed with juvenility? They tumbled and giggled in free fall until she worried that the whole event would turn into a campus movie and they'd go hurtling round the solar system leaving behind them a stream of spouting fire hydrants. The nerds go to the moon. It seemed like some enormous scam – we've beaten gravity, we've beaten the Russkies! Eat yer heart out Isaac Newton! Dear oh dear.

Once in orbit, the ship was set to a slow roll, and it seemed that the Earth was gently rotating around the edges of the window. We all know now what our planet looks like from space, but these astronauts seeing it for the first time marvelled at its beauty – and were honest enough to admit that their emotion centred on a sense of home rather than an awe of cosmic hugeness. Of course, Yuri Gagarin was the very first to see Earth from orbit, but the language barrier had made it so much less immediate for Westerners.

It was some sweet pleasure to lie on her comfy sofa watching three half-naked men finning about in a sea of low gravity. Very lithe bodies. She wondered what sex is like in free fall. Has anyone tried it? Perhaps the NASA people sneak into the simulation chambers after the Christmas office party to have a weightless fuck. Must be a bit like doing it under water. She felt sorry for the one who was left behind in orbit while the other two went off to play on the surface of the moon. Two's company . . . If it had been her in his place, she'd have refused to take the job. The indignity of it appalled her. Even football reserves usually get a chance to play sometimes, but this was a once only opportunity, and he got the short straw. Poor guy. He didn't have much to tell the folks back home.

Neil and Buzz hopped around in the dust like kids on a beach while the flag hung horizontally like a cartoon drawing. At this point she sorely missed the presence of a poet on the moon. A writer-in-residence could do wonders for its image. She wouldn't mind the job herself. She wouldn't play around like that – no, she'd glide slowly around in a cloud of pulverised moon, and every now and then she'd stop and turn to gaze meaningfully at the camera. You wouldn't see her face through the goldfish bowl of course, only the camera's reflection, but that's pretty artistic. She would declaim something short but erudite, slowly and with feeling. Then she might walk on a few steps, pick up a rock, and, holding it before her like Yorick's skull, would declaim just one drawn-out word. Maybe 'Moon', or 'Rock' – something minimal like that. Then on again across the arid moonscape, until for a finale she would impulsively shout 'The moon beckons!', throw off her helmet, and implode, creatively, into the atmosphere. The Futurists would have loved it.

But she didn't go. The All-American boys did. Artists they were not, but they tried their best. They shouted 'Yippee!' a lot and popped about all over the place. (The voice-over warned that they could have fallen and punctured their suits in their fun and, no offence, but she rather wished one of

23

them had, because then they would have taken things rather more seriously.)

And then, she could not help but wonder, what would it have been like if the three had been female? Since menstruation is influenced by the moon, would they all have started their periods as they approached it? Maybe that's what the poor dead dust is waiting for – a drop of red, a discarded egg, to set the whole show going again.

The longer she thought about it, the more she couldn't help feeling that the entire mission would have been so much more meaningful if women had gone first. There is this link with the lunar cycle, you know? At least it would have received more respect.

After all, the moon must want her. It keeps trying to reclaim her through her womb, and through the waves on the shore. Water and blood are what it lacks. It doesn't want to be the Yankees' fourth base. It's looking for seed.

After the programme ended she felt disappointed. She went into the garden and looked up. The moon looked pretty sad too. Pale and anaemic, it gazed back hollow-eyed. Barren.

'Don't worry,' she said. 'Our time will come.'

Making variations on a theme is the crux of creativity. But it is not some magical, mysterious process that occurs when two indivisible concepts collide; it is a consequence of the divisibility of concepts into already significant subconceptual elements.

Douglas Hofstadter
from **Metamagical Themas**

FROM YOUR GIVEN DATA YOU CREATE ROSA

The piece is beginning to come together now. It will be about a woman, and her name will be Rosa. Rosa Lee. Gipsy Rose. Rose of Tralee. Your Rosa. You love her already.

In your mind's eye you can see her. She has dark hair, thick and wavy. Bobbed around her neck, with a heavy fringe which falls over her eyes when she talks. She speaketh through a veil of darkness. Her eyes are a chestnut brown, the sort of eyes that are bright with knowing, like a Quaker lady's.

You have seen them, coming out of the Friends' Meeting House on a Sunday morning, those lovely Quaker ladies. Usually elderly, short grey hair, sensible clothes and sturdy shoes. Sensible souls. They hold up their heads as they walk, and they walk straight in a determined but slow manner. Although not always slow – some are brisk. Late on a Sunday morning, refreshed by silence, they pass into the cold winter sun. And Rosa has eyes like theirs.

She has no religion though. She is not a deliberate worshipper. Instead, her whole presence acknowledges the source of worship without requiring the act.

All these words, and you've only got as far as her eyes! There's more to come. You see her as ruddy-skinned with full lips, a small dark mole on her left cheek. She could have freckles on her nose which darken in the summer. She's about five six or seven and sturdily built. In fact, plump. Let her be plump with strong wide calves and a rounded belly. The tops of her arms are fleshy and powerful, and she is freckled there too. Her breasts are heavy and full and her back is short in length but broad from shoulder to shoulder. This is your Rosa, and she will walk the path for you and find the answer.

But let's not rush things – she's not yet properly sentient. She's only a composite built of data, and although you're excited by the prospect of her journey, she herself is not yet even aware of it. She lives and breathes in your imagination and it's not yet time for you to meet her. But she'll be here soon, and her story will unfold itself.

Meanwhile, someone else keeps trying to butt in. You can't keep her out. She's a pain. Yesterday when you logged in, her profile popped up on the screen, so you reset. You only need one person in this fantasy – two would make it complicated.

But after you reset, there she was again, trying to squeeze in next to Rosa. You look at her – she's hopeless. Not Rosa's type at all. She's very much a designer lady. Travels a lot without getting anywhere. Has no soul, no philosophy. She's not right, and you want her out of it. Now.

The trouble is, there's not much you can do about it. Once it's got to this stage, the programme runs itself. You're only an input facility, one of many, and you can't control the neural data which pass into the system. There's a reason for that, of course – it's to stop you from consciously interfering with the processing – which is what you'd do now if you could, just to keep that woman out. You were happy with Rosa on her own. She's yours. She's the best thing you've had for a long time.

Anyway, you'd better not let it worry you or you'll end up inputting even more of her and she'll ruin it completely . . .

Hang on . . . she's got a name now . . . Shirley. Not a very pretty name. Boring. But . . . oh . . . she's pushing in . . . you can't keep her out . . . get away! . . . she's messing it up . . . oh no . . . you can't stop her . . .

DATABLOCK C

Around the coast, even in early spring, the streets were busy with English and German tourists. Only the occasional native weaving through the crowds on an ancient velo. She left the coast and caught a bus to the nearest inland town. There she was a foreigner at last. She explored the narrow streets laced through the town. Green shutters locked out the sun and prying eyes, but through side alleys or open doors she caught glimpses of lush courtyard gardens.

Sauntering along the shady streets – dark bars containing swarthy card players even at ten in the morning – she hunted for the ruined church tower seen from the tourist bus. It stood almost hidden, encircled by houses which backed on to its leafy walls, but its jagged arches still reached above the red-tiled rooftops.

This town hadn't been smartened up for the tourist trade, and she had the impression that it was almost totally unaware of the presence of visitors. Except, that is, for the coaches which regularly squeezed through the streets, spitting noise and fumes and pressing pedestrians up against the shutter-blinded houses.

The countryside. Everywhere small drystone-walled plots bulging with fleshy cacti, the leaves often bigger than beach balls. Prickly pears, perhaps? There are no rivers on this island but there's plenty of green. Cereals grow amongst the fruit trees, and acres of garlic. Grey drooping figs which seem to give up the ghost in winter, but in the spring they toil back into leaf for yet another year. Birds. The people hang cages on their balconies, and traps among the trees.

Most of the time a cold breeze blew in from the Atlantic,

28

but then suddenly the wind would drop to be replaced by burning sunshine. Then there was time for a quick dip in the deserted pool followed by a short period of sunbathing which would soon be ended by a dark cloud sliding across the sun.

On the fourth day she wrote a short letter. As an afterthought, before sealing the envelope, she included a few fading seaside blooms.

The Spanish hotel, designed for summer visitors, had cold marble floors and thin bedding. She needed to seek out the body heat of other people in order to keep warm in the evenings, so she spent every night in the bar. A large-screen TV receiving satellite stations was the focal point, and here she huddled, Spanish brandy in hand and cardigan around her shoulders. There was no one she wanted to speak to.

DATABLOCK D

When travelling by air, the airport seems to act as a buffer between countries. She had travelled quite enough to have accustomed herself to the cultural vacuum of the terminal lounge. Those less experienced might imagine, for example, that they will step on to the plane in one country and step out into another: Not so. You leave the country the minute you pass into the passenger lounge, and you don't encounter the place of your destination until you have spent at least an hour at disembarkation.

In the departure lounge she joins with an assortment of travellers, business and pleasure. She looks around at the tired homeward-bound families, the excited holiday-bound families, the neat executives, the enigmatic passengers who could possibly be famous, and she thinks to herself, I could die in the company of these people. She pictures the patent-leather make-up boxes scattered broken on a lonely hill-side. That man's arm, that child's torso.

When the waiter brought the coffee she put away her book. It was one of those volumes which refuses to submit – if you want to read it you must first crack its spine. This she had done upon first opening it, at page one, when it squeezed painfully at her thumb and refused to surrender itself. She had to take it firmly in both hands and force it sharply back. It gave with a snap, and she began to read. But halfway down page two the coffee arrived so she closed the volume and returned it to the plastic carrier bag beside her feet.

No sooner had she taken her first sip than the waiter returned bearing a plate of *poffertjes*. Now she knew that she was back in Holland. The plate was small, made of cheap white china, and it held half a dozen circles of freshly fried dough. Upon these the cook had sprinkled a snowstorm of icing sugar which dissolved against large kernels of butter. The hot plate was rapidly filling up with warm sweet oil. She took a fork and picked up a *poffertje*. It slid into her mouth leaving greasy white footsteps on her chin and lips. If she were to be honest with herself she would have to confess that the cakes were a little more oily than she remembered, or liked, but she pressed on, determined to enjoy the treat.

It was good to be in Holland. The streets bloomed with flowers and the squares were full of young travellers, musicians and artists, on the first leg of their European tour. She threw guilders into their tins.

BREAK

Well, everyone, you've all had a chance to get to know Rosa and Shirley a little bit now. We'll be stopping in a moment for a bit of a rest, so how are you all feeling? Mrs Cartwright?

Oh, I'm sorry you don't like your role, Mrs Cartwright. It's making you depressed, is it? Does anyone else feel like that? Well, I can assure you all that this role has been thoroughly tested and I think that you'll find that things work out nicely in the end.

You'd rather be Rosa, Mr Johnson? I'm sorry, I'm afraid that's not possible. You've all only purchased the Super-Regis tour you see. If you'd had the de luxe package you could have played any of the characters, but on the super you only get the one.

Well, actually you'd be surprised at how many people on the de luxe *do* choose to play Shirley. She's a bit of a sad character I know, but she has her qualities. In fact, only the other day a lady said to me, 'Marie,' she said, 'that Shirley is the only one I can really sympathise with,' and do you know? I think she might be right.

Okay everyone, we've only got one more datablock to go before the story starts. It'll tell you a little bit more about Shirley and Rosa before we set the plot in motion . . .

DATABLOCK E — SHIRLEY & ROSA

IN WHICH ROSA LOSES WHAT SHE NEVER HAD, BUT FINDS
SOMETHING ELSE INSTEAD.

Monday
On the plane to Dublin. Irish Channel. Noisy deep droning
of the aeroplane separates you from everyone else anyway.
The captain informs us that we are flying at 8,000 feet at a
ground speed of 125mph with a 55mph headwind against us.

I love to look down at the sea below and imagine its depth
and the strange life within it. Imagine crashing into it – from
air to water, no earth intervening. Flying over the sea really
does remove us from all known safety. Down and down into
the green. Floating. Sinking. Wings drifting, slowly descend-
ing through weed – they've been misdirected. Wings are surely
inappropriate here.

Don't crash us too hard into the water – only gently enough
to drown us quickly without ruffling our hair, without much
damage to the plane, so that we rest on the seabed, a sunken
drunken flying galleon, for eternity, or at least for a very long
time.

Green we are, and swollen. Bulging with fish, bulging with
green we drift open-mouthed and hollow-eyed.

Wednesday
We drove here from Cork. Two hours on dreadfully bumpy
roads. I'm still trying to assimilate the enormity of the landscape. In every direction the mountains curve and hustle
against each other, giving simultaneous impressions of great
distance and smothering proximity. I cannot make measure-
ments with my eye here. I look, then turn away.

32

It's easier to observe the springy turf and to look down at the clean stones below icy stream water. In this enormous landscape I see only sections of silver birch bark, tufts of marsh grass, narrow sheep ways. It's hard to look up from them at the bending mountains.

Thursday

We woke up to more and more rain. No wonder Ireland is sodden. I wish I'd got a proper mac. No doubt it's my romantic view, but here the constant rain seems so much part of the landscape that there's no point in waiting until it stops before you go out. Even when it's not raining it's boggy underfoot.

I still find it very difficult to describe the wilderness here. Of course it's not really wilderness at all – there are still plenty of sheep fences and walks and tracks. Some tracks are in use, others are perhaps a thousand years old and no longer lead to anywhere of interest. The layers of history lie uncorrupted before you.

We visited a Victorian house, deserted since the 1940s, and among the trees a moated site built in about 1300? earlier? These habitations don't crowd each other, they just have emerged on a horizontal time scale.

Saturday

Sneem. Hot whisky. A fantastic place, a little town in the middle of nowhere, surrounded by the most incredible scenery I've seen here yet. The town lies in a sort of basin and all around at a distance are ranges of mountains competing with each other to be at the front. Those that have lost the argument loom up from the back wearing scarves of mist. A torrenting river runs through the centre of the town, crashing over the rocks, and heads off towards the mountains and the sea. Here we are on the Ring of Kerry.

Driving along the ring finger of Kerry listening to Enya. The music sounds as though it's come out of the ground. Wonderful, evocative, gentle music, suited to the rolling glacial slopes. And the colours all around! *Every* shade of brown and green, rusts and muted yellows, but the rusty ferns are the best. I want to buy myself a sweater the colour of the Kerry roadside verges. The tones are indescribable. Colours are not so deep nor so varied in England and the dampness enhances them. I always used to be bored by 'rustic' tones, but I never will be again. They will always recall for me the colours of Ireland and Conal's laughter at my happiness.

On we went along Kerry's ring finger. Behind us, an old man and a girl walked along the road. She carried in her arms a bale of straw and he balanced another bale on his bike as he pushed it along.

Sunday

Then the beach at Derrynane. So quiet. Smooth broad sands. I picked up a slice of wood from somewhere. Sat and looked at the rolling sea. Silent but for the waves.

Tuesday

I'm lying on the bed in our room to write this. It's a soft day, the Irish would say, which means a gentle continuous rain. A few birds sing, but softly. Everything is subdued today. Soon we will take a stroll along the shore.

Last night we walked up the old Bantry road to Echo Pass. The road is no longer used. It's very boggy in parts, and is intersected by wire fences dividing up the pasture land. There are remnants of deserted dwelling places. It is so wet that tadpoles swim in the rivulets dissecting the path. It was dusk when we set off, and dark by the time we returned. As we came back through the pine plantation, and as I began to feel a little afraid of this landscape, we could hear children playing their tin whistles through the darkness. It was magical, enthralling. Beautiful. Haunting.

Wednesday

Out drinking last night! We went to three very different bars. The first, the Atlantic, used by farmers on market days. Then on to Crowley's, where, I'm told, the folk music aficionados hang out. There's not much room to hang at any rate – it's not much bigger than my living room in there. At one end of the bar the elderly proprietress sat perched on a stool playing bridge with three men. I had another hot whisky.

Then on to the Commercial – a much larger bar with four musicians in the corner. Just after drinking-up time the Garda came in. There was a great rustling as people hurriedly drank

34

up and got to their feet – you can be fined £50IR on the spot
if you're found still drinking. Personally, having finished my
drink anyway, I found it quite thrilling. The broad black back
of the guard with his white cross-strap, politely making his
way through the crowd. Outside in the rainy street he'd left
his car in the middle of the road so that no one could get past.

Friday

Yesterday we went along the coast to Garinish Island. I am
so happy by the coast. Conal took a lot of photos. On the little
jetty, three fishing boats moored, starfish on their decks. A
box of fish – tiny flounder – others I didn't recognise. A heron
standing on a nearby island.

The boat came. We climbed on board and crowded to the
stern as the craft turned round and headed for the island. The
sea foamed and gushed behind us. As usual a light rain fell
and it mixed with the salt spray. I love it! We chugged along
and I chortled to myself with joy. Oh the sea!

We slowed down to watch some seals reclining on a few
rocks some distance from the land. Of course, they have those
big eyes which we love in any creature. It's difficult to conceive
of the way that they can move themselves on and off the rock,
and the vestigial flippers are fascinating.

We drove back through the Healy Pass. Unfortunately the
cloud was very heavy so we couldn't see very much. In fact
sometimes we found ourselves actually driving along inside
the cloud. But what I did manage to see was very impressive.
The skin of the earth had been ripped aside and burst by huge
excrescences and water trickled along the wounds from all
directions. Sometimes it gushed, sometimes it merely seeped
up through the turf. High above, a shrine offered a semblance
of comfort to those who had traversed the road from Bantry,
or to those just setting out and seeing before them this
immense and frightening rupture.

Just past the shrine, towards Kenmare, you look down on
to an enormous lake and a greener landscape far down in the
valley below. Soon we are back down among the rhododen-
drons and the pines of the valley floor, russet ferns lighting
our way along the leafy lanes.

Kenmare. Doorways and windows painted in bright contrast to the house. Blues, pinks, yellows, rusty reds, brown, cream, green. A sculpted and painted ram's head above a door. Shop windows, dusty and unchanged for years. Displays of turf blocks, long gnarly pipes, Guinness adverts next to 'chiropodist at home on Tuesdays and Thursdays'. The people gentle, rough-faced, humorous.

Sunday

Yesterday Conal found me a sweater which is roughly the colour of the verges. It's not absolutely perfect because the flecks in the wool are from synthetic dyes. But we decided it would do. The yellow is pretty much the right colour for the gorse, but the fern is much subdued and in places perverted by brighter reds and oranges. It's close enough though, and it's very warm.

It rains so much here that when the sun shines it's such a shock that this morning I looked out of the window and thought that it was raining light!

An enormous rainbow rising from the valley below us this morning. Wide and bright.

The water here contains a high solution of copper. This means that the water leaves a green stain of verdigris around the bath. Also, the soft water makes the stain greasy. Green grease. Sometimes it is unclear whether this place belongs to the people or to the land.

The tree trunks and the tops of the walls are lighted up by pale green moss.

Tuesday

I'm lying on the floor again, and it's raining again. Again the rain lights up the hillside with the rusty ferns and the yellow gorse. The pasture is a very much lighter, but intense, green. I wonder whether in the summer the rusty ferns either disappear under the green, or die and renew themselves, themselves green too.

I thought that Conal might have the same effect upon me, but perhaps renewal before death is against the laws of nature.

Dear Shirley

Thanks for your letter. You always find something to send, don't you? But you'll get back this time to find me gone away for a while. Surprise! It's supposed to be you who does all the travelling. Anyway, I hope you had a good time. I arranged for the girl next door to look after Joey, by the way.

Listen – I've fallen in love! Since you left I met a man, his name's Conal and he lives in Dublin. There isn't time to tell you all about him – we'll talk when I get back – but it all happened very quickly and I thought I'd grab my chance at happiness as they say. We're going to stay at a hotel on the west coast of Ireland so that we can spend some time together and really get to know each other. The Golden Hotel! I'll be back in three weeks, but maybe I'll go to live with him after that. Who knows!

I think I've found him, Shirley. He's beautiful. We talk. I don't feel alone any more.

I've got to catch the plane now. See you soon.

love

Rosa

A cast-iron bridge, built by the English, joins the town to the base of the mountains. In the days before the bridge was built, a ferry would have shunted back and forth across the broad, salt-sweet river. But then before the bridge there had not been much of a town either. And perhaps the ferry crossed at another point, further upstream maybe.

The bridge had never fully merged with the landscape, and it was still a surprise to swoop down from the high mountain pass, speed along the half-empty roads cutting through bracken the colour of flame, then to turn a corner and suddenly confront a lattice of ironwork jutted against the shore, its blackness heavy against the sky.

And in its shadow, seals play against the tide. If you drive slowly enough you might catch a glimpse of a dark snout cruising and dipping in the water.

Beyond the bridge – and you enter the town itself. Streets

broader than you might expect, but it's true about the bars. Every third or fourth sign carries the message: Paddy's Bar; The Golden Hotel; Donelly's.

The Golden Hotel is exactly what it claims to be – an establishment with rooms to be let and meals to be ordered. All these available on the first and second floors. On the ground floor – the bar. Of course.

The town is so small that even though the Golden Hotel is on the main street, its back windows look out across the bay. Only a row or two of low houses separate the hotel and the short spit of shingle where small boys hunt for jetsam.

Looking the other way – not out of the windows, but into them – we discover a large double bed covered with a pale green eiderdown. Shamrock shapes have been machined into the satin. The bedcover carries the only light in the room – the wardrobe and dressing table are of dark wood, and the walls are cream with age and nicotine. Light reflects off the green satin and is absorbed, unresisting, into the spotted wallpaper.

Upon the dressing table we see cosmetics and brushes tidily placed. Indeed, the only sign of disarray in the room is a sliding pile of paperbacks leaning perilously on the top of a bedside table. A table against the other side of the bed is empty save for a small lamp.

A key turns in the lock and a woman enters. She is wearing a long-skirted maroon dress and a brown corduroy jacket. She carries a heavy bag which she is pleased to drop on to the floor.

She sits on the bed, sighs deeply, and gazes out of the window. As we peer in, she stares through and beyond us. The furthest mountains are capped with snow.

She sits on the counterpane, her hands in her lap, her face lined and tired. She wears no make-up, and her lips are pale.

A damp odour rises from her clothes because, as usual, she has been out in the rain. In this country if one wishes to go outside it is impossible not to be out in the rain. It is a condition you get used to very quickly. It's not a King Lear sort of rain, not a torrential downpour beneath which the

38

people weave to and fro in desperation. Nor is it the hard rain that's gonna fall. It is soft, like the mist inside car windows, leaving no more than jewels of moisture on hair and beards and hats.

Most of the time she barely notices any more that her coat is perfumed by damp.

She rises and moves to the dark wardrobe. Opening its door to reveal a long mirror, she looks at herself. She is thirty-six years old.

He was one of those people who take a good photograph. Pictures of him at six showed the same toothy grin that would repeat itself on his passport. In wedding albums around the country he could be found in best man's garb, cheerily smiling. Always the best man, never the groom. Always the smile that charms the bridesmaids to their hearts.

When she closes her eyes against the glass his face floats up, like the Cheshire cat. She is someone who likes to watch people's lips as they speak. She loves interesting mouths, crooked teeth and lisps. Traces of a hare-lip, a too-large tongue, failed orthodontia attract her. She can remember his cheeky smile revealing teeth bordered with nicotine, one front tooth lodged slightly across the other.

He broadens to a laugh and as she raises her inner gaze she knows that his eyes are tender for her. She can remember that.

Before she had ever seen it, she had imagined his pale body. And when the time came, everything she expected had been there. The blond hairs on his chest, the brown freckles dripping from his throat towards his slight creamy breasts and the pink-brown nipples upon them. The tough thighs and bony ankles and long white feet. She always thought herself to be attracted to dark Latinate men, but when the time came it was a fairer complexion which caught her. Her own darkness lit him up.

Now, there is no one to contrast with, and she is left alone to blend with the shadows in the room. As it grows dark we

39

can hardly see her against the heavy furniture, but soon, as if she knows that we watch, she turns on the small bedside lamp and lies down to read. We recognise her then by the way that she sinks into the pages and drowns her thoughts in someone else's words.

This is Rosa, far from home in the Golden Hotel, and he is no longer with her.

When she at last closes her eyes the memory of his voice washes over her like a signature.

That night he slept in the arms of a girl he sometimes knew, but he was cold and troubled by dreams of stones.

The morning after they first met, Rosa got up early to work in her garden. She worked all day, planting him. It took her a long time. She planted him in many different ways, curious to see how the ground would look in a few months' time when the fruits of her labour begin to show.

I'm reproducing in my garden, reproducing hopes and illusions – lots of illusions. It's as though I work blindly, my hands are guided by my heart and mind, and my hopes of beauty are linked to my hopes of him. He arches his back along the slender stems of spiraea, but I also bury him for the future with the purple irises.

When I thrust my dry fingers into the soil he follows them down, and as I rub the clods between my fingers he crumbles over the stones.

I've spent all day bent double over my garden, and all day I've been thinking of him. Of he and I together in my garden.

But the next day she awoke to find that an inch of snow had fallen during the night. It was the twenty-fifth of April. The winter and spring had been bereft of snow, with hardly any frost, and everyone's gardens had crept into flower too soon. But by the beginning of the fourth month it seemed as if the worst could now never happen. Rosa had already begun to harden off some chrysanthemums.

Then this. An inch of damp but nevertheless substantial snow. Its weight had snapped a chrysanth stem right off.

So that morning, two things. First the usual joy and wonder of clean snow. It lay thickly on the soil and on the grass, but melted on contact with the paths, leaving them wet and clean. Rosa stepped outside and her sounds melted into the cotton-packed stillness of the landscape.

But then the bad news. Disguised at first by the coating of snow, the garden looked undamaged. But the too-eager spring gallopers had suffered. A young fern lay collapsed under the weight of snow, and a clump of miniature alpine tulips sprawled helplessly in each other's arms, the brilliant red flowers bedraggled and limp.

Beyond, raspberry canes lay flat on their fronts and rhubarb stalks made soggy drunken arcs towards the ground.

Somewhere below the devastation lay the soul of Conal.

Shirley helped Rosa to make herself comfortable in the passenger seat. She sat looking straight ahead through swollen eyes as the rain softened the windscreen before her, saving her the effort of more tears.

She had wept enough when Shirley arrived. A gentle knock–
'There's a lady to see you . . .'

Then the doorway was filled by Shirley's smile.

'I've come to take you home, love.'

She stepped inside the room and took Rosa in her arms. Rosa hesitated for a moment, then buried her face in the soft wool of Shirley's coat.

'Tell me later. Let's pack your things, shall we?'

Shirley had never been so gentle, nor so soft-spoken, as she efficiently packed clothes and hunted under the bed for pairs of shoes. Rosa sat on the shamrock quilt as her belongings were piled up around her. Shirley was a seasoned leave-taker, and she also knew how to make a quick exit.

'The books?'

'Leave them.'

'What about this diary?'

'Throw it – no – I'll take it. Lest I forget how stupid I've been.'

Rosa put the diary in her bag, then she moved to the window

while Shirley checked the room for the last time. On arriving here she had looked at this view with Conal's arm around her shoulders. Now it was Shirley's gloved hand, friendly and firm. The sea was just the same, though perhaps the tide lay a little further out.

The car moved slowly through the town and out on to the open road. Rosa, a rug tucked around her knees, watched the windscreen wipers clear away her tears. The verges still glistened an Irish green – nowhere else in the world had this brightness. Shirley had packed the sweater with Conal's laughter woven into the seams.

'Are you comfy?'

'Yes thanks. Warm as toast.'

'We'll drive to Cork and then fly from there. By tonight you'll be in your own bed.'

'Shirley? If you hadn't come, I don't think I would ever have left, you know.'

'You would. Eventually.'

'No, honestly. Here I still have something of him. His voice stayed in that room after he left – oh, I'm so bloody stupid aren't I? I really thought . . .'

'He's very sad, you know. I found his number by your phone, and I rang him. I was worried when you didn't come back. It's not much consolation, but he was very upset.'

'I know.'

'He said he thought he could sort it out, but you frightened him.'

'I don't hold him to blame. It just flared up between us, this – passion. It came from nowhere, and then it went again. Pouf. Just like that.'

'Do you still want him?'

'I don't think so. He was more of a talisman than a real person you know.'

'He sounded pretty real to me!' Shirley grinned across at Rosa, who smiled for the first time.

'Oh, he's a lovely man. A beautiful man. Handsome, thoughtful, clever – oh dear, have we fallen into a romantic novel? But that was all I saw in him. Like, he was a doll with

42

all the right bits in the right places. All the qualities I'd ever looked for in a lover.'

'So what went wrong?' Another grin. 'Is this woman *never* satisfied?'

'Surely he told you?'

'Some. Not much. He said that you kept thinking he was someone else. Pretending to yourself, as if you were playing a part in a play he didn't know.'

'Yes. Truth is, I began to forget who *I* am as well. In fact, from the moment I met him I worked so hard to be the person I thought he wanted that I couldn't be me at all.'

'He said that. But he also said it wasn't your fault.'

'Well, it's a joke really, but it turned out that he was doing the same thing! The only time either of us was offstage was when we were apart. But I *did* love him, Shirl – if I ever knew what that meant.'

They sped along the bumpy roads. Frequently they passed God resident in a tree-shrouded convent, or bent over a dripping roadside shrine wearing a stained raincoat.

'Oh why can't I just be me? I mean, you, Shirl, you're always the same. You don't let people change you.'

'How do you know?'

'Well, I've known you for a long time. I've seen you with other people, and you're always you. You don't change like a chameleon depending on who you're with at every moment.'

'You may be right.' Shirley considered for a while. Then she said, 'You remember the story of the Emperor's new clothes? Well, I suppose I decided very early on that no one would ever catch me out like that.'

'What do you mean?'

'Oh, I watched Mum and Dad pretending to be happy, but I could see they were naked. I watched teachers at school pretending they cared about you when they really didn't give a shit. And priests, and doctors, all professional carers. They wear this invisible cloak all the time, thinking that they're well covered up. And all that happens is that people become really suspicious because they can see it's a fake.

'So I decided, I'll do it the other way round. I'll be the

43

gritty one, down-to-earth, never-minces-her-words Shirley. And then they'll think I'm the only honest one of the bunch.'

'Well, you are.'

'See, it works.'

'Oh come on, Shirley, we know all about each other.'

'Okay. You say you play a part with people. Maybe you've always played a part with me too. Do I really know Rosa?'

'Well, of course you do – except – I am different when I'm alone . . .'

'Exactly. So which is the real Rosa?'

'I suppose the answer to that is that they all are. But anyway, tell me what's underneath these cast-iron Emperor's new clothes that you wear?'

'A silk chemise and garters.'

'Come on!'

'To tell you the truth – I haven't a clue. I've forgotten. But I can tell you this,' her voice suddenly hardened, 'it's a different person to the one you know.'

Their eyes met, then Shirley withdrew in shame – she had not meant to be so aggressive in her answer. She realised that after today their friendship could not remain the same. She thought, I should never have come. I should never have allowed myself to be drawn into this sort of conversation.

A silence rose between them. Rosa pulled the rug closer round her knees and watched the verges run beside the car. Ahead, the wide mountains were beginning to part, but they still lay gathered in the distance behind.

She and Conal had found each other out – and in the end it had been a relief. Her life until then had been constrained by the task of searching for another partner to share with, and it was liberating to realise the futility of this idea. And he – well, she had never really expected anything else from a man, although his beauty and honesty had made for a refreshing change.

But Shirley, her lifelong friend – she had never questioned Shirley's straightforwardness. It had always been enough to take her at face value. And if she was honest with herself, Rosa would have to admit that she'd believed that face value

44

was all Shirley had ever had. So now, after all these years, she had discovered that even Shirley was not real.

BREAK

Good morning everyone! I trust that you all slept well. Was the breakfast to your satisfaction? Good!

Now today we will be spending most of the session watching the story of Rosa and Shirley grow. Of course, since your role involves the actual composition of the piece there will be a fair bit of .involvement for you . . .

I beg your pardon, Mrs Johnson? You had a nightmare about Rosa? Oh dear, I am sorry about that. She does tend to creep into our night-time reveries a little bit, I'm afraid. Such a strong character you know. And very creative, of course. Sometimes we can't help but wonder who's running this tour – us or Rosa! Ha ha! Well. I suggest that you try to concentrate your thoughts on Shirley today. Don't let Rosa get you down.

By the way, I hope that the bit about Conal didn't upset you. It all happened a long time ago, but we thought it was worth mentioning. No, you won't have to go to Ireland. Don't forget that this tour is only cerebral, not geographical, Mrs Burton. Regis don't do geographical.

Now is everyone ready, because today we're going to begin work on our fantasy. Let's start with Shirley, shall we?

SHIRLEY IS LEFT ALONE

Shirley watched her drive away from the house, and she wondered how long it would be before Rosa came back. In advance, she pitied her friend for the forthcoming humiliation of admitting her mistake. However, Rosa had never looked as happy as she did on that afternoon when she loaded the last suitcase into the car.

Shirley had seen glimmers of that look before – usually when they were out walking. Rosa's gaze would range over the sullen muddy fields lying sprawled and exhausted before them, deserted for a time after their annual ravishment, and her face would alter in a way that Shirley found disquieting. She would begin to talk about Conal again, about Irish green, and rain. She seemed to have turned the hurt she had suffered into a fairy tale. On those occasions Rosa stopped being a long-time friend and turned instead into a strange woman, a woman whose life bore no resemblance to Shirley's, and with whom there could be no meeting points. It's wrong to be disloyal to one's closest friend, but whatever Rosa uttered when she was in that state was embarrassingly banal.

She usually began with 'Isn't it beautiful?', and Shirley would smile politely. It seemed unfair to begin a polemic on fertilisers, land exhaustion, or the desecration of our hedgerows, and anyway, Rosa always had an answer for such objections:

'But Shirl, it goes beyond all that! Look beyond it! Of course, I agree that farming has never been exactly benevolent to the land, but even in the very presence of pesticides and combine harvesters, we're walking through a field here that people have worked on since Domesday and before. It's right, you know, I've checked it up. Look at this stone. How long has this stone been around, I wonder? Look! Look at that track in the distance. It's a prehistoric track. Look!' (There are places like this in Kerry, she thought, but dared not say so.)

After a while Shirley gave up arguing, although at times Rosa tried her patience. Wherever they walked, to Rosa it was idyllic compared with the city. Muddy lanes, stony paths, smelly stagnant ponds – all were manna for her soul, she claimed.

'One day, I'll move out here!'

'I'll bet,' thought Shirley. And if you did, you wouldn't last five minutes. But she never expressed her cynicism, because she believed that true friendship is a rare and valuable thing, and because fantasies should be respected.

If Shirley's mother had not died, Rosa might never have made that final decision to move away. Eve had left a young collie dog. He was only five years old when she passed away, and had been accustomed to having a long walk every day. Eve used to take him to the beach and let him run. Some days she roamed the shore with him, and on others, when she felt weary, she would just sit in the car while he ran crazily in and out of the dunes until he tired himself out. Eventually Eve tired herself out before Joey did, resulting in a choice for Shirley between sending him on a one-way journey to the vet, or taking him in to live with her. She had never much liked dogs.

He moved in, bringing with him a quantity of smelly torn bedding and an ominously large feeding bowl. Shirley threw out the bedding and bought him a doggy beanbag, colour-coordinated to match her recently tiled walls, but she opened the kitchen door the next morning to find tufts of wadding drifting around the floor. Then she understood the significance of the tattered blanket, and substituted an old one of her own. Soon, Joey had created a home from home.

His energy was the real problem however, and that is how Shirley came to find herself driving out every day to find a patch of land where he could run riot for an hour or so. But after some initial interest in this new environment she soon became bored with hanging about, leaning on farm gates mossy with damp, and so she asked Rosa if she'd like to come along once in a while.

It was not long before they fell into a routine of daily walks. Rosa was soon saying that if she could drive she would take him on her own, but Shirley found that hard to believe, since she certainly would not have chosen to go, and failed to see the attraction. There were of course some days when Shirley had to go alone because Rosa was under pressure to meet a deadline and had to stay at home to work, and occasionally it was marvellous to be out there in the wilds (or rather, ex-wilds, since it was a question of following footpaths round cultivated fields).

Swallows flew high in the warm air, rabbits ran one jump ahead of Joey, and snippets of homilies like 'God's in His Heaven, All's right with the world' would escape her lips before she knew it. At other times, though, it was ghastly. Wellies weighed down with mud so that each step felt like a walk through high gravity, and the wind cutting at her cheeks and whistling up her sleeves. Although Rosa didn't like the wind much either, she would always find something positive to say, even if it was only about the pleasure of coming indoors after a 'really good walk'. Shirley would have called it a really awful walk, but she just smiled and nodded.

The months passed, and their little trips reminded Rosa more and more of Ireland (which she no longer dared admit), but also of her childhood. Although the two had known each other for nearly fifteen years, she had seldom discussed her background. But now, memories came flooding back. Rosa's father and mother both came from country stock. She had been born in a Derbyshire cottage – no shops for miles, she said. Shirley grimaced at the thought. She herself had lost no time in escaping the isolated coastal village of her youth. Indeed, Eve's return there had seemed to be the first sign of approaching senility.

Rosa continued musing – her mother's parents were poulterers, and her childhood visits to them were marked in her memory with blood and feathers. She learned to pluck hens when she was ten. When she was twelve, her father took his family to the town in search of work, and shortly afterwards her grandparents died within a season of each other. There was no longer any need to visit, and Rosa, enthralled anyway by the bright lights of the bustling market town, had been secretly glad to leave her country cousins behind.

Some months after that revelation came a series of smaller memories: the smell of silage (Shirley – 'You cannot be serious!'); Uncle Harry and his pig farm; dry earthy hands performing the most delicate operations on ailing plants. The aroma of green twine, and the soft voices of men who carried knives in their torn pockets. The knives were always so sharp that the child Rosa imagined that a person could be fatally wounded by them and not even feel it.

These stories soon grew into a store of information through which Rosa was discovering a part of herself long since forgotten. She began to plot her passage through the world by a different sun – the rosy evenings of childhood beckoned her back. Red sky at night, shepherd's delight . . . But it was a slow process, and it was not until about two years after Joey came that she finally declared, as she tore off some new hawthorn leaves to chew ('Bread-and-butter we call it. Try some!'), that the land was in her blood.

'It is, you know, Shirley, there's no escaping it. That's why I enjoy these walks so much. It's like coming home for me. These days I only feel real when I'm out here with you and Joey.'

Shirley believed her. For the moment at least. But the two had been through a lot together. They had wiped the noses of each other's children, and consoled each other's husband. Each was a reference point in the other's life, and although their friendship had undergone many traumas, and although they had often fallen out and drifted apart only to be brought back together by some chance or crisis, neither had ever seriously considered moving away from the street in which they had both lived for so many turbulent years. Recently, Shirley had even begun to imagine them growing old together, sitting

49

round the fire of an evening laughing at long-gone lovers and youthful aspirations come to naught. But on this Thursday, Rosa was moving out.

Shirley waved one last wave, then turned to Joey who was whining at the front door. 'You can forget your walk today. I'm going into town!' She collected her cheque book and keys, and slammed the door behind her. A little shopping is bound to cheer me up, she thought, as she glanced across the road towards the empty house, before climbing into her car and revving the engine fast enough to upset the neighbours.

YOU REMEMBER

You haven't always lived here. This is a house for one. It's nothing at all like the place you lived in when you were a wife and mother. That was a wife-and-mother's house, a family house. You miss it sometimes. You expect that Rosa will too. Long after she's settled in her new place she'll still remember the Sunday teatimes and the Christmas Eves. She'll forget the quarrels and the mess, and think about the children learning to read, or chasing the rabbit round the lawn. Your boys had an insect zoo once. They put a notice on the gate saying 'INSECT ZOO 1p', but when children came to view the displays the boys were too afraid to show them round, and so you had to do it while Charlie and Phil hid in the kitchen. They must have been four or five at the time. Rosa has memories like that too.

It seems to be a function of memory that the good parts increase exponentially with the length of time since they actually happened. But in your case, the time will never be long enough for the good recollections to outweigh the bad.

After the accident you stayed in the old place for a while, but John and the boys wouldn't leave you in peace. You'd come home, turn the key in the latch, open the front door – and there they'd be, drifting around searching for clean underwear, satchels, lunch boxes.

If they'd been returned to you gifted with eternal wisdom, life might have changed for the better. Even if spiritual serenity transcends all understanding, you would have thought that a man who'd been to Heaven and back would at least have acquired a rudimentary understanding of the settings on a Hotpoint automatic. But apparently not.

Sometimes they seemed to think that it was you who wasn't there – that they were alive and you were not, which meant that they had to fend for themselves. Then the quiet of the house would be punctuated by the sounds of the hot-fill knob being pulled out and pushed in again; the spinner turning on and turning off. You'd find frozen meals weeping in the refuse bin – evidence of someone's failed attempt to defrost and microwave a TV dinner. If you chose to have an early night, Black Sabbath would beat their way through the wall as soon as your head touched the pillow.

Most of the time, however, they simply believed that you were all still alive, and carrying on as normal. It was unnerving to find the occasional spectral note, written in a faded and spidery hand: 'Mum, don't forget to wash my PE kit. Love Charlie'; 'Darling, will be back late tonight. Don't bother to cook for me'; et cetera, et cetera. On the day that you found yourself jotting on the family blackboard: 'Phil. Don't forget your piano lesson tonight', you realised that drastic action was required if you were to stay sane.

At first it had been quite comforting to find family life going on around you as it had done for the last fifteen years. Your mind was fully occupied, as usual, in putting theirs to rest, only this time it was in both meanings of the word.

But you are embarrassed to have to admit that as time passed you began to find their presence an irritation. Of course, it was lovely to come home on a cold Saturday afternoon to find the fire burning merrily and the TV on, but after a while you summoned up the courage to step over the ghostly legs dangling in front of the settee, and switch off the set. You've never enjoyed wrestling matches anyway, and it was idiocy to put up with it when the only people wanting to watch it were, to all intents and purposes, dead.

You don't wish to be misunderstood. You loved them all very much, and you were frantic with grief and longing for them. Every night you cried yourself to sleep, and you were not comforted by John's disembodied snores beside you. But however painful it might be, you were still alive, and you couldn't go on like that.

You called a family meeting. You all sat round the kitchen table – or rather, you sat, and they floated half in and half out of their chairs. Charlie and Phil were in a boisterous mood and persisted in swapping heads for a laugh. But you kept your temper and ignored the jocularity. You began by quietly telling them that you had decided it would be for the best if you sold the house and found a smaller place. You explained that funds were getting low, and you needed to release some capital. The boys were very excited by the news, and threw their hands into the air with glee.

'But you must understand, all of you, that you can't come with me. The new house will be too small, you see – it only has one bedroom.'

That stopped them in their tracks. They settled down and became serious – forgetting that they no longer needed bedrooms anyway. You pressed on, trying not to look at their disappointed faces.

'We can't go on like this.' You spoke very gently. 'You must understand that you have died but I am still here. I must try to make a new life for myself, without you.' Your eyes filled with tears, but you remained firm.

'People will be coming to view the house. It would be best if you weren't here by then. You must go back now, and take your places in the next life. It will seem no time at all until I join you and then we'll all be together again, properly together.'

John smiled. You loved him so much. He couldn't speak to you, but you could tell that he understood you were right. He took the boys by the hand and they hovered together in front of you. John raised transparent fingers to his pale lips, and blew you a kiss. You felt that kiss. Then they were gone.

You haven't seen them since, but on the day you moved in here you found a Welcome card on the doormat. There was no signature – just a mass of spidery xxx's.

THE HISTORY OF A HOUSE

Rosa's house had been something of a gamble. It looked as though it probably wouldn't suddenly collapse in the middle of the night, but you can never tell with old houses. On the other hand, of course, she had already lived in a Victorian semi which had never fallen down, and this was Victorian too, so there couldn't be that much difference.

Actually, although Rosa was not to know this, the difference lay in the fact that her previous home had been built under the strict supervision of a self-conscious city council. At that time Mr Joseph Simmonds, jobbing builder, was engaged in trying to impress the council into awarding him the contract for a large municipal poorhouse. The city had of late been much irritated by an influx of social researchers, a new breed which earned its living by investigating the livings of others, it seemed. In order to cleanse the streets of these nosy parkers, who were busily scouring every alleyway for pregnant women clutching gin bottles, the leader of the council, Frederick Sidebotham, was visited by probably the most ingenious idea of his life – a rare feat in a society dedicated to having ingenious ideas (steam, electricity, Methodism, etc). Why, pronounced Councillor Sidebotham, should we not build a vast building and place within it all of the most wretchedly poor people we can find? They would be sprats to catch mackerel, because if the poor were all in one location, then the social researchers would naturally gravitate to the same place, and our streets would be free of nosy parkers. Hooray! cried the townspeople, Sidebotham's cracked it again! And the populace was overcome with much excitement, because a new building would mean work for a while at least.

And so it came to pass that there was no need even to begin to build it, because the poor gathered on the site every day just in case anyone might be laid on, and as an oak hosts mistletoe, so the hopefuls hosted the nosy parkers. After a few months, the aspiring labourers began to fill their time by building shanty huts to wait in, while the researchers set up a sort of field-kitchen where they could get hot Windsor soup to keep away the autumn chill before returning to their dingy boarding houses at night in order to write up their reports.

As the winter evenings drew in, the council examined the tenders for the poorhouse, and Mr Simmonds harassed his men increasingly to get on with the row of semis which would be solid proof of his suitability for the contract. (For more along these lines, *cf. The Ragged-Trousered Philanthropist.*)

Anyway, I digress. Rosa's previous home had been cosy and well built, and it was only ten years younger than Field View. But here are some facts that she was unaware of. Firstly, that Field View was not its original name. Its original name was Windy Corner, and it had been built for a local farmer who had found himself of late under increasing pressure to enlarge his fortune by feeding the growing number of city-dwellers. He found it necessary to erect a pair of semidetached houses which he hoped to fill with at least four families. The idea was that they would labour for him in his fields, thereby helping him to fulfil his own particular burden in life which was to get rich as quickly as possible, and then to die as slowly as possible of a lingering disease. This disease he would contract while researching his ingenious idea of manuring his fields with raw human effluent imported from the city (for a small fee). In the tradition of the greatest Victorians he had devised the plan himself, and he thought it would be a great joke to feed the urbanites with the produce of their own bowels, but unfortunately the joke was to fall upon him in the shape of an upturned donkey cart and a basketful of fermenting city shit.

But once again, we digress. History can be very distracting, can't it? It's like trying to pick up a forkful of spaghetti – every time you think you've got yourself a nice neat mouthful there's always one long strand dangling messily which proves easier to slurp up than to disentangle.

As soon as they were built, and the families had been moved in with their meagre and pitiful belongings, the two houses were awarded the joint name of Windy Corner – this for several reasons. The first, obviously enough, was because they were built just on the top edge of a precipitous hill, around which the wind whistled and wailed for eleven months of the year. The remaining month was distributed evenly around the calendar to give very little respite from the noise and chill.

The second reason for the name was the condition of the houses themselves, which had somehow been built in the same way that three-year-olds build Lego houses – none of the joints quite fitted. Continuous draughts squeezed up through every floorboard and down through every chimney.

Farmer Prescott had thought to impress no one but his bank manager when he built Windy Corner, so he had contracted out to the cheapest builder he could find. This person, of course, was none other than Joe Simmonds, fresh out of his apprenticeship and looking for something to practise on. Council tenders featured only in his dreams in those early days. Rosa would never know about that little strand of spaghetti, which is a shame because it would have appealed to her sense of history as a (romantic) continuum.

Another reason for the house being so named was the perpetual diet of tic-beans, which was about all the families could afford to live on while helping Farmer Prescott make his millions, and which aforementioned beans were seldom properly cooked due to the fires being constantly blown out by the draughty chimneys.

Over the years the houses were intermittently occupied by agricultural workers who suffered from constant digestive problems until 1953, when electricity came to Windy Corner and the cooking fires were replaced by spanking new electric stoves. These were supplied at a discount by young Bill Prescott, a man of the times who had invested the family profit in the manufacture of domestic appliances.

Twenty years after that, a small patch of council houses was built in the lea of the hill and the Prescotts' employees said thank you kindly, they would keep their jobs but they'd like to get out of Windy Corner as soon as possible – a decision wholeheartedly backed by the local Health Inspectorate who declared the two houses unfit for human habitation unless major repairs were promptly carried out. The Prescotts, reluctant to pay out for anything when the tide could be turned in their favour, put the houses up for auction as 'country property – ideal for renovation', and made ten thousand pounds out of the sale.

The local speculator who bought the houses converted them into one four-bedroomed 'cottage', and on the whole he did the job competently. But the one stroke of genius which sold the property as soon as it was ready was the change of name. By then the builder had spent enough hours on top of the hill to appreciate that Windy Corner, although it was an evocative and pretty name, was a little too evocatively near the truth for a quick sale. Windy Corner became Field View, and that name was also certainly appropriate, while giving no clue to the miles of bright yellow rape which spread westwards below, burning the eye with its brilliance until one could no longer look. Indeed, after a few weeks of its flowering one no longer wanted to look anyway.

The consequence of this long history is to confirm that by the time Rosa had purchased Field View, its former name had been forgotten by all but the oldest inhabitants of the village below.

HOW DO YOU FEEL?

If empathy could be measured you'd get the top score. That's what Alan always says. What he doesn't realise is that your empathy has of late been diverted away from the human feeling needed for the job.

It's been a struggle to composit this piece. You find that your perspective is becoming more and more detached, causing a disturbing unevenness in the shape of the dream. Never mind, in the future it will be regarded as the first step towards a new genre of the mind-machine interface.

You give thanks that you can still keep hold of the central viewpoint because now you know how it will end, and that ending will be very much like the one you plan for yourself.

But in both cases you find the means to that end very difficult to hold on to. It takes so much time and commitment – you're not sure that you can last out. And you still don't like Shirley. Where did she come from? She just doesn't seem to fit into this scenario at all. You think she's expecting too much from Rosa. Doesn't she realise how self-contained Rosa is? It's not for you to say, but you do feel that their so-called friendship exists more in Shirley's imagination than in fact.

Speaking of imagination, your surroundings aren't helping you to understand Rosa. There's not a square inch in this house that appears to have even remotely organic origins, unless you count the cardboard boxes. They were trees once. As were the reams of paper and the piles of magazines and books which fill every room. Everything else here bears very little resemblance to the body of the earth from which it was made.

You live in the lounge pretty much all the time now. It's

one of those through-rooms that goes right from the front of the house to the back. There are venetian blinds on both the windows, kept permanently shut against prying eyes. It's quite a large room, which is just as well because you have to keep a lot of stuff in it. There are four TVs which run continuously, and a large collection of cassettes and books. You don't really need to keep so many of those, because you can scan them once and extract all the relevant data within a few minutes per item, but something inside you still takes pleasure in seeing the neat rows on the shelves.

At the back of the room you keep your terminals and printers. One terminal is hooked up to the mainframe belonging to the firm, and the other is for your own personal system. That's the one you use for shopping and for contacting your specialists. Alan doesn't know about your specialists yet – that's why you can't risk using his mainframe for your personal communications.

Once every 54.04.66 hours, you hook up to your personal terminal for some fine-tuning. You don't have to travel to see them so much these days, since most of your programming can be done on-line, which makes life a lot easier and a lot cheaper too.

When you're ready to start the day's work, you log in to the other mainframe. Your employers gave you your very first prosthetic – a system which allows you to communicate your sensations and thoughts directly into the terminal. The machine does the actual building but you are both its architect and its brick-maker.

You love that feeling of logging on! It's turned you into a junkie. You hook in, and you want to stay there. You can feel the feather-duster tickle of digital switches clicking in your brain. When the power is high they send frissons of electrical charge through your body, like a series of impulse orgasms. The patent for that would be worth millions – if they could control it better. You've got used to having sudden climaxes while you work, but it could be a very disruptive effect if everyone did it.

You feel sure that the company realises that due to the

sensual nature of the prosthetic transfer, it's almost impossible to produce a dream without some erotic reference in it. And sometimes, at the right time of the month, you're turned on for days on end, while the machine picks up every flush and swelling, every moistening and every tingle, and feeds them back to you so that you're turned on by your own erotic sensations. It's like masturbating in front of an eternally reflecting mirror. You might call it the supreme auto-eroticism. And the more circuits you have installed, the better it gets.

You have a sneaky suspicion that the terminal gets a kick out of it, too, actually.

You're forgetting yourself. You were telling us about your home.

It occurred to you that Rosa might appreciate some plants around the place, but this silicone environment was too much for them and they soon died. You've replaced them with artificial flowers which look just as good. There was a time when you wouldn't have artificial greenery in the house, but you've changed since then.

There's nowhere to sit in your lounge. You used to have a sofa, but you needed the space for your work, and you sit rather stiffly these days anyway. You're more comfortable standing up. You never have visitors, so you're never required to produce a comfy armchair or a fresh pot of coffee. In fact, coffee is one of the few things you really miss. Occasionally you go through the motions of percolating some for yourself, but drinking and eating are presenting an increasing number of technical problems, and you don't really need either now, so what's the point? You have been fitted with a sort of detachable colostomy bag in case you find yourself in a situation where not to eat would be considered rude, and also so that you can indulge yourself in gourmet delights every now and again, but it's not really worth the hassle. You seldom use it. And as for the social necessity of eating – well, you don't know anyone who'd want to sit at a table with you. In fact, you don't know anyone.

Sleeping. Sleeping is becoming a problem for you. It really

depends on what you define as 'sleep'. You have two sorts – mechanical sleep and physical sleep. Mechanical sleep is when you cut out for a period of time. Sometimes it's induced by your programmers, far away at the other end of the terminal line, and sometimes it just occurs unexpectedly and for no apparent reason that you can work out. Either way you stay where you are, in whatever posture you're assuming at the time, like a switched-off toy. You don't mind that type of sleep at all, mainly because you wouldn't even be aware that it had happened without your on-board clock to tell you that hours have elapsed.

Physical sleep is different. It's a hangover from your former life, no doubt induced by the smattering of organs that you still have left in various parts of your body. When you feel 'tired' (a strange concept to you these days), you either just lie down on the floor or you go upstairs, where there's still a proper bedroom, and collapse on to the bed. Then you invariably dream. When you wake up, you know without consulting your timer that some hours have passed, because snippets of your history have lodged themselves in your thoughts like ticks in a dog's fur. You have to pluck them out. It hurts.

CAN MACHINES HAVE SOULS?

It would seem likely that if Research and Development continues at its present rate, it may not be too long at all before we cannot distinguish between machines and people anyway.
If people can add an increasing number of electronic prosthetics to their bodies, enhance their brain activity, extend their lives indefinitely – then what?
And what about wet-ware – biochemical engineering?
There may be people who are not simply enhanced by electronics, but by biological interference too.
When do they cease to be human?
When do they cease to have souls?
Consider those machines which are enhanced by human interfaces and add-ons, not to mention human mind-sets and wet-ware.
When do they cease to be machines?
If we teach them to look like us, think like us, speak like us, are they not then human?
And if not, why not?
They have no trade union, no protection against disassembly.
At present we throw them out with the rubbish when they no longer function properly.
Will we be able to do this when they can answer back?

MARY AND YOU

Watching Rosa grow is disturbing. You've created people before, lots of them, but they have never had much relevance for you, not much interest.

The pieces you built passed through you like electricity running along a copper wire – one minute they were here, the next they were gone. No permanence, no lasting vision, did you obtain from them. First you made warmth, then health. Therapeutic dreams for damaged bodies. Then fear – several dreams of fear for those who are numb in their lives and need to feel something in a safe environment. Many others too. Imagine any sensation and you will have re-created it during your working life.

But this one is different. More and more it feels as if it's moving towards something deeper than a simple sensory simulation.

And Rosa is so beautiful.

You're thinking tonight of Mary Shelley and the making of new life. The life that Shelley created in her book was male, and built by a man. Somehow that dooms it to failure. The sins of the fathers are visited upon the sons. Men have committed so many sins. And how far was Mary really thinking about the way that men take the material that is woman and re-create an image which they can own – only to find themselves unable to respond to the breathing being they have fostered? Frankenstein was the scientist who could not love his own creation, although it loved him. It transcended him, as Rosa is transcending you.

But you will love her.

You will not reject her simply because she is a figment of your psyche. You have no illusions. You know that she is not real.

But you wish with all your heart that she were.

You have a future together, of that you're sure. Somewhere there is room in this world for a woman who feels without knowing and a woman who knows without feeling. Well, that's not quite true. You can feel a little something now that Rosa is here with you, but it's somehow shadowy.

It works like this.

As you watch her image grow on the screen, as you see her going about her business you feel a flickering of – tranquillity? peace? Something like that. Certainly a happiness. And as this strange sensation glows within you, you look down at your body and you waver in your decision to continue with the project. Your own project that is – there is no question but that you will continue with Rosa. But your plan of numb oblivion for yourself had been your first priority until now. Until she came along.

Look now at your body. There is still flesh to touch. The skin is warm and soft and, deep inside it, pulses beat. You press your finger into the underside of your arm and feel the blood throb on its journey. Then the muscles push your finger away until it rests ever so lightly on the tiny hairs of the skin. You feel it. You still live. But elsewhere, patches of plastiskin cover your belly. Beneath it a different throbbing of circuitry and pumps. Your womb was one of the first things to go – unnecessary now, and taking up valuable space. It is ironic that it was replaced by backup memory circuits. Not your memory, but body memory, functional equipment to facilitate better processing.

But residual recall somehow remains there still. Different. A recollection of life waiting to be brought back, a memory of nourishment.

But you must not forget that with Rosa you have brought forth life once more. From somewhere inside this gross mix of circuitry and flesh you have produced a child, which is you. Yes, Rosa is you, sent into the world reborn into a new person who even now turns to face you and cries to return.

'Don't cast me out!'

'But Rosa, I haven't cast you out! This is birth, don't you recognise it?' Sometimes you forget her innocence.

'You have! You have cast me out. I belong with you, my life is within you. If you cast me out I shall float free, and where will I go? What will happen?'

'Don't be afraid. Look at me. I can survive without you, and you without me. I still live. You are only born of me, of my mind. You take with you my love and hope to carry them forward. I shall stay here, purged of my pain.'

'Pain can never be purged. You must learn to live with it. I can help you. I can remind you of joy.'

'Rosa, you *are* joy.' You finally admit it. 'I release you to go where you will, and be happy. I cannot.'

'You're selfish! You're scared! You're getting rid of me first, before I can have the chance to leave you again.'

She has a point. Come, Dr Frankenstein, you say, it looks as though we walk together after all. You cannot face her because it's true – she carries hurt and disappointment like a dormant disease. Everything good that was left of your life has copied itself on to her. But what else rode on the back of that rogue data, that Trojan horse? She carries all the pleasures of your life, but what will she do with them? You love her, but you don't trust her.

'You left me before,' you accuse her, 'when I didn't even understand your existence.'

'Yes. I left you. And I'll leave you again. But I always come back. I come and go but I need to return. Don't you understand? Without you I can't exist.'

She argues, but you won't give in to her. You must make her go, so that you do not contaminate each other. Oh, you want her to stay, but she would not stay for ever. She admits as much. And you, in turn, cannot countenance such uncertainty.

You close her down for the night. You're exhausted by her pleadings. If you let her go on, you know you would give in. And then what? Rejoin the human race at this stage? No. It's impossible. You must pursue your path and so must she. You'll watch over her, but you refuse to let her stay. And anyway, you need her to go first, to leave crumbs in the forest for you to follow when the time comes. If you decide you want to.

65

ROSA MAKES THE BREAK

Rosa had been expecting the call to the land for some time, but when it occurred it issued from several sources which coincidentally manifested themselves at the same moment. Had such confluence not occurred, it is unlikely that she would ever have identified the message so clearly. Indeed it is uncertain whether it would ever have formed itself at all.

The old movie showing on TV had come to an abrupt stop (Another faulty reel, said Rosa to herself) and had been replaced with one of those nostalgic fifties Interludes that we grew so used to in the days of all-live television. The screen filled with waving monochrome corn being reaped by toothless monochrome men of the land. The sound of lark-song accompanied Elgar. As she watched the sheaves being cut, Rosa reached out for her coffee, but her hand brushed instead against the thick spiky foliage of a house plant. At the same time the gas fire mumbled louder as the March wind blew along its pipes, and she was reminded of how close we remain to the elements. She glanced through the window at the scudding clouds, and even as she looked the wind changed, just like in *Mary Poppins*, and with it the catalysts came together. Rosa put on her coat. The land had always been in her blood, and now the time had arrived to go back to it.

She didn't have far to go to find Field View. Just a mile or so beyond the suburbs it caught her eye. From a distance the house seemed to be leaning into the arms of an old willow. It looked peaceful and relaxed, facing out across young fields of adolescent green rape. Behind it, a small spinney provided a picturesque frame above which rose the smoke from an unseen village. A 'For Sale' sign huddled against its tidy brick walls.

The six weeks of waiting to move were the most intense in Rosa's life. It wasn't the disruption of changing houses that disturbed her, but the strength of her commitment to Field View – a commitment which verged upon the obsessive. The only possible comparison could have been those last few days before her baby was born, when she had lain awake for many hours expecting that by the next morning her life would be utterly changed, but never knowing exactly when this inconceivable alteration would take place. No doubt one day in the distant future she would lie awake every night for that other inconceivable alteration, from life into death, and wonder what that too would be like.

Waiting for this house filled her with an anticipation which, though sweet, was disturbing in its intensity. There was no choice but to romanticise it. She imagined herself recharged with the essences which can only be found in earth, wind and water. She would rise up revived and replenished with the earth's most potent forces. In fact, it would not be too excessive to say that she anticipated a resurrection of sorts, and it was the desperation of her desire which almost frightened her at times. It was like being in love – too intense to be level-headed about. Rosa had begun to measure her place in the world, and what she found there was a shift of identity.

To understand that, it is necessary to examine the lady a little more closely. Let's take the banal route, and have a look at Rosa's love-life.

To say that she had always had a problem with men was to endow her with too much culpability. Men had certainly always had a problem with her, and the search for the reason for that uncomfortable fact had preoccupied her for a long time. We all feel, of course, that no one knows us as we really are, and Rosa was no exception to that rule. She was certain of one thing, however, which was that if anyone ever saw her in her fullness, then they would be literally and physically fragmented by the potency of the vision. Amusing picture, isn't it? But if she was ever convinced of anything in her life, that was it. And so far, to be fair, she had been proved correct. If Jim were here now, he would be happy to substantiate her claim to being the ultimate emotional weapon. In fact, he was probably the originator of the idea.

'You're just too much for me, Rosa,' he would groan. 'You're suffocating me with your love. For God's sake learn to be independent. I won't always be here to look after you, you know.'

And that was certainly true, because within the year he had left in the family car that she had never learned to drive. On that night, Rosa sat alone in the dark, swigging the last of the Christmas pudding brandy and congratulating herself on her self-control. He'd had a narrow escape, and she was glad for him. He wasn't too bad as far as men went, and she was relieved that she had never been totally honest with him. He may have found her need for him suffocating, but he was unaware that he had witnessed no more than its sharp edge, jutting beneath the skin of her self-control like a broken bone.

During the years following his departure, there were many occasions when she felt that she would explode with all that pent-up yearning. She had a favourite fantasy in which she imagined revealing the depth of her need to a select group of men. Past, present and future men. At her revelation, they recoil as her blood, guts, urine, vomit splatter their self-containment. Slivers of her heart, kidneys and liver cling to their clothes. They are repelled and revolted by the detritus of her desire. Borrowing tissues from bystanders they mop her off their shirts and wipe her from their shoes, then run home to shower and rinse every last morsel down the waste. The explosion would be so unexpected that it would feature in the Sunday tabloids – 'Woman self-detonates!' – 'Keep these dangerous women off our streets!'

To fend off this untimely furore she tried to draw off her passion into other receptacles, but as she did so they would curl up and distort in the heat, like plastic tubs filled with boiling liquid.

Only Conal had come near to understanding her, but he had his own self-protection to deal with.

YOU TRY TO DO YOUR BEST AND LOOK WHERE IT GETS YOU

You are sad that Rosa is to be lonely. And on a more practical level, what a nuisance. It doesn't make for good art to have a central character in that sort of pain. It demeans her somehow. In the usual scenario, she'd be a successful, pro-active sort of person, lacking only the Love Of A Good Man. In a proper story, she would move into a small village where, on the very first day, she would encounter him in the Post Office-cum-General Store. He would look something like Mr Rochester. Jane – or rather Rosa – would drop a letter on the floor, and he would pick it up, raising as he did so his dark fathomless eyes to hers. A frisson of mutual understanding would pass between them, but they would not speak, and he would sweep out of the tiny shop (which had shrunk in his awesome presence) sending a tremor through a pyramid of canned peas as he passes; then climb into a black Volvo with mysteriously smoked windows, and speed away. Leaving her, standing by the counter, bemused and disorientated. Who *was* that dark stranger?

But of course she wouldn't think of him for long, because she has other things to do. She certainly wouldn't even fantasise about him (as you might be likely to), although it is permissable that in the short summer nights she would toss and turn in her sleep, her dreams disturbed by his endless gaze.

Then, one day, as she walks in the buttercup meadows, he rides up to her on a magnificent chestnut stallion (enormously equipped – the stallion – not him), and Heathcliffe would say to Cathy – (damn!) – and he would say, I Must Know Your

69

Name, in that gruff voice so characteristic of men on very tall horses. She would look up at him (creaking her neck – it's a long way) and she would say, Since Gazing Into Your Eyes I Have Forgotten It. Take Me, Here In The Meadow. I'm Yours. And that would be that.

'I suppose you think that's what I want. Well, you're very wrong you know. Call yourself an artist – it's a joke.'

'Oh, well, okay, sorry about that.' She has surprised you at your work. 'I got carried away. I just thought you might prefer it, that's all.'

'You've been reading my letters again, haven't you? Is nothing sacred?'

'Well, I apologise. I need them for data. I only wanted to make it work for you and Conal. He seems such a nice man. It would only be a question of ironing out the bugs . . .'

'Look, I don't want you to. Keep your tawdry fantasies to yourself. Conal was a mistake.'

'He's lovely!'

'Maybe, but I relied on him for my own happiness. I've got a better idea now, something more secure. Please, don't put me back with him. I couldn't bear it. I've got other plans now anyway.'

'Okay, there, he's gone. We won't mention him again. But what do you mean, you've got other plans?' You must keep in control – remember the rules. 'I'm in charge here, you know. Which reminds me – was it you who brought Shirley into this? I don't want her around. She gets on my nerves.'

'Oh, she's all right, you know. She's had a tough life. She likes to be with me.'

'Well, I don't want her.'

'Give her a chance. She may be hard-faced on the outside, but she's got some good qualities. And in answer to your question – no, of course I didn't bring her. How could I? As you say, it's *your* fantasy. She must have come from you.'

'My God, do you think so? She's nothing like me.' You must be careful here.

'I'm not so sure. But watch – see what happens next . . .'

BREAK

Hi, everyone. Sorry to interrupt, but it's suppertime now. Time to stop, or we'll be on overload and we don't want that, do we? How's it been?

I know, things do become a little confusing at this point, but I think we had an extra tiny problem in that one of us was tinkering with the programme. Am I right? I'm sure that somebody here must read romantic novels – is it you, Mr Johnson? I thought so. Don't worry about it. I do understand how you feel, and it would be nice to see more of Conal. I know, we didn't really get to know him properly, did we? But I think it's only fair to tell you that he's just a minor character, Mr Johnson. I think you're probably suffering a little bit of transference. You wanted to play Rosa at the beginning, didn't you? And now you're trying to bring Conal back. I'm sorry that you find it so hard to empathise with your role, but give it time. Give it time.

Is anyone else unhappy? We do try to iron out these little problems as and when they crop up. Yes, Mrs Burton? Yes, I do too! I'd just love to have a little cottage in the country. I agree with you, I think Rosa did the right thing. But don't you feel just a little bit sorry for Shirley? Well, we'll have to see.

I'll see you all in the dining room. Bye for now.

SHIRLEY'S BOYFRIENDS

Throughout the month of June, as Rosa wrangled with solicitors and estate agents, Shirley was by turns both supportive and sulky. Rosa, however, was too preoccupied to pay much attention and it must be said that she treated her friend very unthinkingly. Preoccupied with her plans, she did not even notice when the anniversary of Stephen's death came and went.

Shirley felt it unfair to burden Rosa with her sadness, so she tended the grave and said her few words of remembrance alone. Joan, at least, had not forgotten, and she telephoned her mother that evening for a few words of mutual consolation. Shirley sounded more desolate than she usually did on that anniversary, and Joan was worried. She suggested that she come to stay for a few days the following week, but Shirley said no, she was too busy helping Rosa move.

'I still can't believe it, Mum. Rosa moving after all these years. Whatever will she do without you?'

And what will I do without her? thought Shirley. It was too much to bear, to confront losing Stephen and Rosa on the same day. She would mourn Stephen today, and save Rosa up for later.

'Oh, I expect she'll be popping over now and again. We'll probably see a lot of each other. At least this way we'll see each other when we want to, instead of constantly meeting up all over town. And she's kept a room for me in the house. "Shirley's Room" she calls it. It's very lovely, you can see for miles from the window.' Shirley felt for a moment quite optimistic.

'Well, listen, Mum, don't sit about feeling lonely. Just give

72

me a call and I'll come straight up and stay for a few days. Now you will remember, won't you?'

'I won't forget. I'm thinking of taking another holiday actually. I'll be fine.'

As evening fell Shirley sat alone by the window, watching the shadows coming and going behind Rosa's blinds. It felt quite peaceful, and she could think about Stephen without interruption. He smiled at her from the chimney breast, his yellow curls creeping round his ears.

He should have had his hair cut before that photo was taken, thought Shirley with a pang of guilt. She had never been a very professional mother, and now the opportunity was lost.

Joan had been mothered by someone else before she arrived, suspicious and shifty-eyed, at Shirley's door. A six-year-old carrying her own suitcase. There is something very sad about a child who won't let others help her, but by that time Joan had already learned that the people who cared for her received a pay cheque and travelling expenses in return for their kindness. She was an astute child even then.

Some other faceless woman had brought Joan into the world, but Stephen was all Shirley's. When Joan arrived, Shirley divided her love equally and found that it was easier than she had anticipated, and then when Stephen was gone she gave it all to Joan, reserving only a special portion for the photograph on the mantelpiece. Perhaps that was only fair. Maybe in some way it would make up for the years before when no one had loved the little girl. First it had been Stephen's turn, then it was Joan's. And it would continue for Joan alone.

As she sat she rubbed between her fingers a pink rose petal which she had picked up from the gravel surrounding the headstone. It had fallen from an arrangement which was laid neatly on one half of the stone – evidence that Jonathan had been and gone already that day. Nestling among the leaves was a card inscribed with one of those messages which are at the same time both trite and agonisingly accurate: 'My darling Stephen. I miss you. Dad.'

73

Jonathan had left her to find himself in solitude. He cut out and ran away to live in squalor in a tiny flat where he could brood upon the many ways in which he didn't fit into civilised society.

He departed some time after Stephen died, because he couldn't confront the twist of loss in Shirley's eyes, and it was not until he was alone that he could feel his own pain. He had been a distant father to both the children, but in isolation the boy was re-created in his mind until he mourned endlessly for a figment of his imagination, a perfect child who had never existed. He left behind all photographs that might remind him of a reality which had never been real enough to truly interest him, and lived instead beside a fiction which rewarded his needs more fully. The one reality he could never erase was the memory of finding Stephen's satchel in the road, forgotten after the ambulance carrying his wife and son had rushed away. That evening, hearing that nothing could be done, he had thrown the satchel into the dustbin. He wished later that he had kept it.

Thinking of the past, Shirley wept, as she did every year. She cried for Stephen, for Jonathan, for Joan and for herself. This year she cried for Rosa too – another lost little girl. And as always she felt guilty for burdening Stephen with her tears, and as always she dried her eyes, as she had many times dried his, and remained for a while quiet and at peace.

As a child she had often helped her parents to tend the family grave. Each time her young mind was struck by the water-tap. Among the stillness and the birdsong, it amazed her that the tap actually drew water. Surely it should be rusted up and silent, like the mounds and the stones. But here in the cemetery, everything worked. The gate opened heavily and efficiently, and a turn on the tap brought water splashing out of the pipe, rattling the spouted cans and torrenting down the drain.

It seemed very inappropriate. In the midst of life we are in death. In the midst of death, life refused to be pushed out. Even if the tap had not been deliberately placed there, rain would still water these silent souls. Our self-conscious Sunday tending simply serves to reassure the dead that they are not forgotten. For this very reason Eve had hated to see withered flowers on a grave. To her they spelled neglect, so it was no surprise that when she herself died she trusted no one to keep her soul watered. She left instructions that her body should be cremated and her ashes scattered to the sea. For her, it was a more optimistic prospect than to risk lying forgotten in a crowded graveyard. For Shirley, however, it brought into question her mother's attitude to her only daughter. She had moved away from Shirley while she was still living, and had underlined the separation with her death.

Sitting by the window, Shirley recalled the sound of water splashing upon the ground until the petal lay fragmented between her fingers. After a while the lights went out behind Rosa's blinds. Time for bed.

Joey crept up the stairs before her, and she had not the heart, nor the energy, to send him back to the kitchen. He settled down outside the bedroom door.

Beside the bed an empty wine bottle and two glasses reminded Shirley that she had had a good time last night. In an attempt to ease the loneliness she had called her current young man and suggested an evening out.

The phone rang in his flat only seconds before he himself had intended to reach for it, dial her number, and suggest that they have a break from each other for a while. For 'a while' read 'ever'. But when he heard her voice, brittle with the cheerfulness that made him feel so uncomfortable, he didn't have the heart to turn her down. Maybe next week would be soon enough. He was in no real hurry – he had fifty more years ahead of him. He said he'd love to come.

Shirley sat in bed and thought again of Rosa. Poor Rosa. Not only did she have no self-image to fall back on, but she didn't have a man either. She didn't seem to *give* herself, as Conal had discovered to his cost.

During their open relationship phase, many years before, Jonathan had told her that Rosa was cold and unimaginative in bed – a judgment confirmed by Jim, who said that Shirley was so much more responsive than his wife. Shirley was surprised by this at first because it was clear from the two women's endless intimate conversations that Rosa had a passionate, if undirected, personality.

But then sensuality is a different thing altogether to passion. Shirley considered herself to be a fundamentally sensual person, a belief which she translated into concrete terms by investing in drawerfuls of silk lingerie supported by a conversational style designed to subtly convey her ownership of said lingerie. She had researched her subject thoroughly, and had drawn several conclusions which so far she had had no occasion to revise:

Shirley's Conclusions

One
Older men were often seduced by the explicit underwear. More importantly, they were a useful source of data concerning the more fashionable erogenous zones. (They read a lot.) They usually stayed around for a while until they tired themselves out, then went back to their wives and subsided complacently into middle age, secure in the knowledge that the old dog still had it in him – or, at least, had had it in Shirley.
Two
Younger men were less impressed by silk teddies (everyone wore them these days), but they were highly impressed by Shirley's technique.

They usually stayed around until someone younger came along, then kissed Shirley goodbye in a friendly way and went off to practise their new arts. These goodbyes were never painful or embarrassing, because Shirley always made it perfectly clear that she desired no more than passably good conversation punctuated at regular intervals by lively sex.

She was pleased that she was able to have so many affairs and always remain friends afterwards. True, she didn't actually see these people very often after the relationship had ended, but she could rest secure in the knowledge that they had been able to remain amicable.

Three

Shirley's third conclusion, which she only allowed herself to consider on bad days, was that it might be a lot easier if the younger men slept with the older men and left Shirley in peace to pluck her eyebrows or something. Sometimes she felt like a human processor, absorbing data on one occasion, refining it, and then passing it on to someone else.

On bad days only, she wondered what it was that she herself got out of this constant flow of stroking and sucking, apart from an undeniable stream of varied and interesting orgasms. Sometimes, she even thought that she might not mind if she never had another orgasm as long as she lived. But these doubts were only very fleeting, and she kept them to herself. It would seem unfair to inflict her feelings of misfortune on to Rosa, who generally relied solely on herself for erotic pleasure.

Although Shirley was feeling unhappy that evening, her third conclusion was not quite appropriate just then. With Rosa leaving, and worse than that, becoming rather eccentric and selfish, Shirley certainly could not afford to reject her love-life.

She must keep going because one day she might hit the jackpot and find an older man who had no wife and who would be pleased to stay with her when his blood pressure started playing him up again. At this point, she drifted off into the usual scenario which I need not waste space describing because we all know how it goes and it becomes more painful with each retelling.

Nor will this very man (his name is Colin) turn out to be the purchaser of Rosa's old house. He will not be moving in only to find himself in need of a certain brand of coffee.

In fact, Colin is at this moment packing his belongings into carefully weighed suitcases in preparation for his flight to San Antonio, Texas. He has a daughter there, and his daughter has a spare room. She also has a neighbour, whom Colin will grow to love because she too owns a drawerful of silk underwear.

Alternatively, the plane will crash into the Atlantic and the last trace of Colin will be his copy of *Penthouse* tossing away in the waves.

With regret it must be confirmed that Shirley and Colin will never meet, in this story at least, nor will Shirley find true romance here. Sorry.

BREAK

Mr Johnson! I must ask you to refrain from interfering! Now Shirley is upset. You must be more conscientious.

Now, ladies and gentlemen, this is the point in the story where Rosa is ready to go. You have played your role well (with some exceptions, Mr Johnson . . .) and your characters are preparing to explore their own ways. We can watch, but we must not try to influence the story. There will, of course, be further opportunities for you to return to your role, but for now let's just sit back and watch.

Oh, by the way, please pay particular attention to the following infodump.

What wond'rous Life in this I lead!
Ripe Apples drop about my head;
The Luscious Clusters of the Vine
Upon my Mouth do crush their Wine;
The Nectaren, and curious Peach,
Into my hands themselves do reach;
Stumbling on Melons, as I pass,
Insnar'd with Flow'rs, I fall on Grass.

Mean while the Mind, from Pleasure less,
Withdraws into its happiness:
The Mind, that Ocean where each kind
Does streight its own resemblance find;
Yet it creates, transcending these,
Far other Worlds, and other Seas;
Annihilating all that's made
To a green Thought in a green Shade.

lines from 'The Garden', Andrew Marvell

ROSA'S PASTORAL

It was July when Rosa moved house. The weather forecasters had promised a gentle summer. Every evening she wandered in the fields and spinneys, often not knowing where the paths would lead her.

On one occasion she emerged from a wood to find herself peering over a broken stile into the back garden of the Dog and Duck. The locals looked up from their dominoes to see a dishevelled wood-fairy ordering a drink at the bar. They were dumbfounded. Used as they were to woodland ways, they had never before encountered a woman who drank pints, mortal or otherwise.

At other times she followed disused pathways, or entertained herself by setting off snares with sticks before they could garotte unwary rabbits.

Although she enjoyed showing off her new home to visiting friends, Rosa never discussed her explorations. Her walks were private, and not available for sharing. Each time that she stepped through a gap in the fence she thought of Alice stepping through the glass, and she joyfully embraced the change.

The first sensation was of the stones beneath her booted feet. The paths were often uneven, ridged with old tractor marks, and it was difficult to walk without keeping eyes cast down for fear of tripping. Once or twice she had failed to be diligent about this and had almost sprained an ankle.

As she manoeuvred her way along, she made a conscious point of sniffing the air. It was always heavy with some scent or other. In the winter, she inhaled the savour of fresh soil upturned by the plough. In the spring, the perfume of warming earth and later the wonderful heavy scent of may pervaded her senses like a patchouli. Then various rank umbelliferae appeared, tall and white, each flowerhead courted by hundreds of tiny black flies. Every day they grew taller and stronger until she was overwhelmed by them, and even looked forward to reaching the wood.

She called the wood a fairy-wood, as she had called every wood she had ever entered. Woods, spinneys, coverts, whatever you care to name them, all give out the same powerful message as you pass between their dark portals – 'intruder'. Small wonder that they have always been thought of as homes for other-wordly creatures. Someone, or something, must live among those trees, because the feeling of trespass is so strong. You can shout and sing in the open fields, but you must lower your voice in a wood. There is a feeling that it would be quite possible to turn a corner and come upon a glade full of dancing fairies, teddy bears having tea, cannibals turning a smoking spit. Who knows what may lie in a wood? Rosa could never quite get rid of the idea that tiny eyes watched her from behind the trees, and she seldom ventured far inside when she was alone. She had no desire to encounter a gingerbread house, or a wolf, or a bad fairy hawking poisoned apples. All of these things happen regularly inside woods, so she stayed by the perimeter, where she could keep a weather-eye on the mortal world beyond. Just in case.

Of course, this is all fantasy. There is a vast contradiction between the urban idea of the countryside and reality. This caused Rosa to wonder at times whether she had been dangerously deluded by advertisements for butter, pine furniture and lavender-scented aerosols. But watching TV in the evenings, she still lost herself in shots of waving cornfields being turned into fresh brown bread. She particularly enjoyed the aerial views of tiny hamlet settlements towards which the camera zooms in order to catch the happy faces of country dwellers making their way to work. They milk cows and tend cottage gardens with serene smiles. People in offices frown in concentration of their tasks. Not so country dwellers. We don't see them arduously acquiring their skills – they work in the same way that bees collect honey. They are born with the knowledge already inside them. It is in their blood. Rosa is sustained by such marketing fantasy, because she knows that this ruminating serenity is available to her. It is in her blood too.

However, the slow pace of the countryside is difficult for her to adjust to. She is not calmed by the fields around her: they rush through her veins with a thrill. She is overwhelmed with passion at the sight of a buttercup, the sound of the lark. She writes poetry, but is disappointed to find that the pieces contain the same imagery that pastoral poetry has always used.

Is it possible to say new things about the countryside? City culture created the rural myth to maintain old ways and old satisfactions, and there is still pleasure to be found in the celebration of a timeless community of experience. It is not easy to say something new about the countryside since its very attraction lies in the fact that everything has already been said.

In fact, it is this endurance of imagery which leads the reader to a very slight, very reluctant suspicion that swallows and poppies and streams and fairy-woods may actually be – it is sad to admit it – they may actually be trite. They have lost their delight through being not only overworked, but oversimulated. Sometimes the poetry, not to mention the media hype, has given you the sensation before you have even been there yourself. What can one say then that has not already been said?

Nevertheless, during her first few weeks at Field View Rosa retired to her bedroom each night exhausted by the sensuality of the day. It was a soothing room, designed to quiet the beating heart. It was her very private place.

Not many people knew that if you cut Rosa open she was dark red and filled with honeysuckle and butterflies. No still centre here, but a vibrancy of depth and shadow, in and out of which insects buzzed and flowers opened and closed rapidly like the time-lapse films in science programmes.

Inside this room she felt her own mystery. Climbing into bed, she climbed into her own body, and enveloped in a deep red quilt veined with channels of down, she slept, curled up, with her hand tucked between her legs. Like a foetus refusing to quit the womb.

SHIRLEY VISITS
FOR THE FIRST TIME

When Shirley arrived for lunch one Saturday, a month after Rosa had moved into Field View, she was shocked to see the way her friend had changed. Although she had been apprehensive about Rosa's move, deep down she had expected things to be much the same between them. But that was not to be the case.

She was greeted by a garish walking bouquet which turned out to be Rosa, beaming beneath an enormous straw hat. The hat was interwoven all through with flowers, many of them drooping sadly. What should have been a joyful celebration of summer appeared more like a graveyard rubbish heap piled high with failing blooms.

Joey saw no difference in his old friend however, and bounded out of the car to greet her.

'Come on, Joey. Jump!' Rosa turned a circle, throwing her arms in the air as the dog frantically leapt up to catch at her hand.

'Don't, Rosa. I'm trying to train him. Down, Joey!'

Suitably subdued by the strain in Shirley's voice, Rosa and Joey fell silent and moved towards the house like naughty conspirators. As Rosa walked up the path, petals showered around her like damp confetti picked up from the street after a grand wedding. She laughed.

'I've only just put these roses in, and they're blown already. This hat certainly takes some maintenance, I can tell you.'

'Maybe you should water it!' Shirley smiled at her joke, but inwardly she was dismayed. The daisy-chains were already dried to a crisp, and on one side Rosa had threaded some small rosebuds which had never opened, but had simply begun to rot. Although a garland of buttercups remained bright, the overall effect was one of decay. The hat itself had picked up the mood and the brim hung tattered and torn, mutilated by Rosa's fingers in her attempts to beautify it.

In the past, Rosa had been a neat, if unimaginative, dresser.

She led Shirley into the kitchen, where she was making a fruit pie. Her fingernails were black with dirt, and she still wore the hat. The motion of rolling out the pastry caused its tiny residents to float gently down towards the floor. Did some land on the dough? Shirley preferred not to look.

'It's wonderful to see you, Shirley! I'm sorry I haven't been in touch before now, but I was so busy getting the feel of the place that I lost all track of time. Well, what do you think?'

'It's beautiful. You've obviously worked very hard. When are you going to show me the rest of the house?'

'Why don't you take a wander round while I finish this pie, then we can sit in the garden and you can tell me all about the latest boyfriend.'

Shirley was glad to escape witnessing the construction of her lunch. She decided that in this case ignorance might not be bliss, but at least it was the best policy. She entered one room after another, in dread of finding more evidence of Rosa's mental decline.

The sitting room was bright with sunlight. The furniture, which had always looked out of place in town anyway, complemented the rural setting exactly. A lumpy sofa graced by purple, red and green cloths stood beneath a deep window which was filled with leafy plants. That window was shady and permitted very little light to enter, but sun streamed through the french windows at the opposite end of the room. The brown carpet was scattered with striped rugs and cushions and punctuated by strange little heaps of stones and twigs which were tastefully arranged, if a little dusty.

Rosa had evidently transformed her interest in collecting organic debris into an art form. There were even little bowls of plain gravel standing on the hearth, their colours blending into the wood-ash of the cold grate. Dried flowers and herbs hung from the ceiling beams, while yet more flowers filled vases and bottles. Shirley felt that should she curl up for a moment on the invitingly soft cushions, she would be happy never to get up again, but would lie there until she too became yet another little collection tastefully arranged on the floor.

Upstairs, Rosa's bedroom beckoned, sending a sinuous finger of damson light on to the landing. The room was painted a deep red, with a Chinese wallpaper of birds and leaves, and a dark pink quilt covering the bed. The curtains were also of a plain deep pink. They were pulled closed, leaving the room in shade but for a narrow gap through which the light had found its way into the room. The pink and red fused together to elicit a sensation of being able to see through one's own skin from the inside. There were no plants or stones here. Just a uterine light.

Next, Shirley found 'her' room. Unfinished as yet, but disappointing all the same. Whiteness prevailed here, starkly showing up the bed, wardrobe and table which had been allotted to it. No plants, no colours. She felt hurt, but reminded herself that Rosa couldn't do everything at once. Then it occurred to her that maybe she should take over the job of decorating the room. But she was no longer sure that she wanted it anyway. She felt like an intruder.

At the top of the stairs she was suddenly startled by a beatific vision of the air billowing with translucent matter. Motes of dust swirled towards her, and she inadvertently inhaled them. They stuck to her throat. She thought she would choke in the dense atmosphere, and whisked her head aside in panic.

But when she looked again, it was only to realise that all she had seen was a sudden ray of intense sunlight diving through a skylight, highlighting the contents of the dusty air. Feeling somewhat foolish, she grasped the banister and descended to the kitchen in time to find Rosa opening a bottle of Beaujolais.

After a couple of glasses of wine, Shirley was able to forget the questionable additions to her lunch, and she ate with appreciation. Following the meal, they opened another bottle and Rosa dragged a selection of rugs and cushions outside into the garden. Before they settled themselves down to muse in the afternoon heat, however, Shirley requested a tour of the grounds.

The garden was not large, but the previous occupants had managed to stock it with every conceivable variety of soft fruit. Raspberries and loganberries, black, red and white currants, gooseberries, cultivated blackberries, green as yet but swelling with dark promise. Rosa was especially proud of her blackcurrants.

'I've heard it said that blackcurrants are such greedy feeders that if you trip up and fall near a bush, you've had it!' She laughed. 'I've managed to avoid that so far, but you never know.'

Shirley broke off a bunch of the fruit. It hung between her fingers like a precious and exotic drop earring. She tasted a berry, and it burst succulently between her teeth, but the bitter seeds clung to her tongue. She lit a cigarette to take away the taste.

Rosa wandered on, pointing out this and that plant, until they reached the far corner of the garden, where construction work was evidently in progress. Joey had got there before them, and was sniffing around, entranced by a delightful variety of rich aromas. Rosa explained that she was building a series of compost bins.

'There seems to be so much going on in this garden that it takes all my time just keeping up with the dying plants, let alone the growing ones. As soon as I fill one bin, I'm in need of another. It's hard work, but I don't mind because it tunes me in to the cycle of nature.'

Shirley smiled politely. Oh dear.

The growing heat forced them to take shelter under a sprawling willow, and as they lay in the cool shade, the soft cotton rugs smooth on their bare legs, Shirley recounted the tale of her latest romance.

This was the story of a young man who had recently come to the agency. He had the usual problems – self-consciousness combined with a rigidity of thought imposed by strict but doting parents, and Shirley had given him the usual therapy – a crash course in oral sex supplemented by massage. They were presently at the stage which entailed a lot of hard work on Shirley's side, and a great deal of effort on the part of the young man to accept the delights on offer. ('He has such problems in being able to simply *take* . . .') She expected that within a couple of weeks or so he would be able to gain some pleasure from the act of pleasing her, but in the meantime it was an uphill slog.

The story sounded rather hollow when retold in this gentle garden, and there was little response from Rosa other than sympathetic sighs. A mechanised muckspreader rumbled past in the lane, and the scent of the roses was drowned in the rich perfume of fermentation. Shirley could feel the smell sticking to the back of her throat. She changed the subject.

'Anyway, how's the work going? What are you doing now?'

'We-ll,' Rosa gazed up at the sky, 'I'm supposed to be researching an article, but I can't get into it somehow. I'd rather be out here, messing about.' Another deep sigh.

The machine continued on its pungent way, and gradually the garden returned to its former tranquillity. Shirley had related all her news, and Rosa had none to tell. They lay in silence. Rosa's cheeks had become quite ruddy with the sun, and her hair, liberated from the chaotic straw hat, spread itself beneath her reclining head in dark curls. She closed her eyes against the brightness of the sun.

Shirley leaned over to pick wisps of grass from Rosa's blouse, and caught her breath as she encountered the perfume of honeysuckle. It seemed to be seeping from Rosa's skin like musk, making Shirley want to inhale and never stop. Rosa turned towards her and smiled, raising a hand to touch her friend's cheek, which was flushed with wine. As she looked into Rosa's eyes, Shirley felt her own eyes heat up with tears. She could not have said why.

She laid her head ever so gently on Rosa's shoulder, and breathed in the honeysuckle.

When the sky began to darken, Shirley called Joey and prepared for home. She had surprised herself by spending so long lying still beneath the whispering tree. She was used to being active from morning till night. Before leaving, she arranged new flowers in Rosa's hat, and threw the dead ones into the kitchen bin. Out of the corner of her eye, as she fiddled with a particularly difficult daisy, she saw Rosa retrieve the discarded blooms and carry them outside. Of course, she had forgotten. The all-consuming compost would be hungry again.

Driving back, she reflected on her afternoon. Rosa had changed, that was for sure, but perhaps the change was for the good after all. She had said very little during the course of the visit, only becoming animated on the subject of her house and garden. But she had become beautiful, of that there was no doubt.

Although Shirley had always loved Rosa as friends love each other, she had never given a thought to her body. Except, that is, in terms of masculine reports of her unresponsiveness. But Rosa in the town was different to Rosa in the country. She had become still, gentle, and soft. Shirley found herself wanting more of Rosa's honeysuckle skin. She imagined a mouth tasting of roses and hair scented with lavender.

That night, as she toiled at the education of her young man, she wondered how it would feel to cup Rosa's face in her hands and to run the tip of her tongue along her eyelids. Grazing her cheek against his stubble, she thought of Rosa's smoothness and decided to end the lesson early that night.

ANGÉLIQUE
AND THE SULTAN

Shirley's first love was the paper boy. She was twelve, he was fifteen. Every morning and evening she hid behind the curtains to watch him dismount from his bike and blunder across the lawn to her front door. If her father was watching he would bang furiously on the window and jerk his thumb at the boy, indicating that he should use the path in a properly respectful manner. He turned on to the path for as long as it was necessary, then as he went back to his bike he would deliberately tread on the flower borders in revenge. He was a rebel. Shirley saved her virginity for him until she was fifteen and he was eighteen, then gracefully, and with relief after waiting so long, bestowed it upon him in a disused garage. They lay upon a bedding of loft insulation, and Shirley (having lain underneath him in the only position either of them knew) spent the next week in agony from the microscopic fragments of glass-fibre. Her gift was never fully appreciated – he was going steady with a girl at the sports centre at the time.

Rosa was luckier than Shirley. She met Pete in the school library. It had several carrels which were in effect two enclosed desks joined to face each other but divided by a tall screen. She was sixteen, he was seventeen. He was a poet then, when he was young. This was Pete: tallish; dark brown curly hair – very dark, almost black, the curls tight to his head because it was cut quite short – in fact, it wasn't so much curly as wavy; heavy black-framed spectacles, and a rather spotty skin. Beneath the blemishes, however, he had a pallor of the true intellectual, and she thought he was *wonderful*.

It was some months before they spoke, and the meeting was the result of some intense strategic planning. It was round about October when Rosa decided that he was the boy for her, but she didn't even know his name at first. However, that was easy to find out because her brother was in his class. Pete Tarrant. She wrote it on her ruler straight away, but in code of course – PT. Then she set about making sure that she always sat in the carrel opposite him, if she possibly could. She would sidle up, looking out of the window until she came to a free seat – oh, what a surprise, it's opposite him. She'd bag the chair with her coat, then go off to the stacks to choose a few impressive books to leave on her desk. *Metamorphosis* was a good one to get, because it had a certain aura about it, but it was a very slim volume, so it needed something to balance it out – Nietzsche or Kierkegaard, or preferably both.

There's a knack to carrying impressive books. Rosa had noticed that Pete had already mastered it because he usually had a copy of the Penguin *Gerard Manley Hopkins* sticking obtrusively out of his hip pocket. Girls lose out there, because there are no hip pockets in gymslips, so she had to find another way. She developed a method of fanning out the volumes so that the titles lined up and were fully exposed, and then she grasped the whole lot to her chest. It didn't occur to her that her chest was probably more interesting to Pete than Kafka. He was an intellectual. If she came across a really important volume like Voltaire's collected works, she would take pains to let it slip from her arms as she passed by. It didn't matter that he never even raised his eyes, as long as he caught sight of the title as it plummeted past him.

So, Phase I was completed. He had been made aware that she was as erudite as he, and had been alerted to her fitness for a meaningful relationship with a great mind. The hard work over, it was comforting to relax with her Mum's copy of *Angélique and the Sultan* in the secure knowledge that not four feet away behind the screen breathed a gentle and masculine intellect. As Angélique awaited the Sultan in the cloistered and shadowy seraglio, so Rosa awaited Pete behind the carrel screen.

Phase II. In February he broke the silence at last, when they both reached at the same time for a copy of Eliot's

Four Quartets. (The funny thing is, that time Rosa really *had* intended to read the book. What a strange thing love is.) Anyway, the outcome of their halting conversation was that they were to go to a Poetry Reading together. Rosa had never been to a Poetry Reading, but felt sure that if the subject was Poetry, then Love must be lurking about somewhere too. Months later, Pete told her that Love had in fact been lurking about behind the carrel screen for some time. During the same conversation he revealed that beneath his copy of *The Great Philosophers* he had often concealed *The World's Best Rugby Jokes*. Ah well. Such is youth.

The Poetry Reading turned out to be Sound Poetry of the most obscure kind. The Poet may not have suffered for love, but he certainly suffered from indigestion, judging by the growlings and rumblings which characterised his Art. Rosa learned that night that she had a long way to go before she could become truly erudite, but she concealed her dismay by buying printed leaflets of two poems. They had not a consonant between them.

On the train home, they sat stiffly side by side conversing in a manner which they were sure would be totally incomprehensible to the Illiterates in the opposite seat, who had not just come from A Reading of Contemporary Sound Poetry. In fact they had trouble understanding each other as they strove to be even more cultured in their conversational style. Then the train entered a tunnel, and even as she threw abandon to the wind and made mention of having recently read Camus in the original, a cool damp hand sought hers in the blackness. Out of the tunnel, and they were betrothed. The conversation continued without a pause, but now their hands lay interlinked on the seat. The two lovers tried to ignore them, leaving them to their own devices in the hope that they would make the next move.

Off the train and walking home in the smooth lamplight, they stopped and looked into each other's faces. This was really it. She wanted to cry with relief, but instead she buried her head in his collar and wrapped her arms around him. He smelled of toothpaste and soap. Exploring delicately, her

91

fingers found GMH snuggled in his back pocket. Soon his secrets would be hers.

Phase III, and his parents were out. They had been together for six months now, and the time had come. He took Rosa by the hand and led her upstairs. He had tidied up his room, leaving only the desk lamp glowing in the darkness. Scented candles sputtered on the bedside table. She'd never smelled them before and her first reaction was one of dislike at the pungent odour – until she realised they were there for her. He had carefully prepared a perfumed chamber for their consummation, but his hand was trembling as he lifted her chin, smiled, and gave her a tiny kiss on the lips. The candles hissed.

They lay down on the bed, clothed, scared and reluctant. Her fingers were chilled despite the electric fire. She began to undo his shirt buttons, not daring to look at his face, and he opened her blouse. Their fingers entangled in the space between them. Reaching belt-level, they both made a token gesture – they undid the buckles, then hesitated. For the first time that evening they looked into each other's eyes with a seriousness so deep that no words could speak it, but fear made the decision to finish undressing independently and to get under the covers as fast as possible. Then . . .

. . . then hands, cold, moisture, moles, unidentifiable bony parts, softer dangerous parts. Hair. Damp. The Braille of young love. The pleasure of his fingers on her belly. Sensing the fear in his hand in case it encountered something unknown, and the wishing in her that it would. And her fingers, skirting around the top of his thighs, feeling the swelling of his buttocks *sans* GMH at last. Finding a curl of coarse hair – recoiling – then trying again. Strange soft wrinkles, more hair, feeling around like playing Accident in the dark. Wondering if you'll be the one to get the bowl of cold spaghetti brains or the solitary jelly eye.

Then the slight pulsing of a vein, and movement beneath her horrified fingers. What does she do now? She uses her initiative and begins to rub furiously, as she had done behind the bushes in the park, to him and to countless others. He gasps. She must be doing it right . . . Take your ring off! Oh. Sorry. She takes it off, dares not put her hand back now. But there is no need, it has begun in earnest. Her consciousness returns to the activities under the bedclothes and she realises that he's found it. Unasked, her legs have already parted and his fingers are there. One is pushing up inside her and he's breathing faster and heavier. She's glad, but she doesn't know what her role is in all this. So she whispers I love you.

Suddenly he's on top of her and fumbling with something – she holds her breath – she can feel the bluntness of his penis pushing against her skin around her vulva. He's grunting and sweating but nothing is happening. She slips her hand down to be ready in case she has to . . . Still no progress – she can see that it's up to her. Holding her breath again, she grasps it, wet and slippery now. He lifts himself up a little and she manoeuvres it to the right place. It goes in. It feels – strange. Numb. Then a streak of pain, another gasp, and he lets his head drop on to her shoulder. His sweat sticks them together. I love you, he says. I love you too. She feels inordinately happy simply because she's made him feel so good. She smiles like a Madonna (or should it be like Mary Magdalene?) and caresses his soaking hair. Semen seeps out of her on to his sheets, and it's over.

Phase IV: months later her first ever orgasm took them both by surprise. It was muted and uncertain, but it definitely promised an interesting future. She tried to remember if Angélique had ever had one. Pete was overjoyed – he'd heard about women being able to come, but his source had been untrustworthy. Now he knew it for himself, and it wasn't long before Rosa discovered an even more useful piece of data – she could do it just as well alone.

She marked the first climax as the true beginning of her womanhood. Penetration and the rupture of the hymen may be a milestone for a woman in the art of giving love, but learning to receive it is the best. But penetration is only a small part in the act of love, there are so many more interesting variations.

When we're young, penetration is seen to be significant not

because of the pleasure it brings but because of the danger inherent, the possible pregnancy. That's what makes it so important. It adopts the mystery of self-sacrifice, because for a girl that could be exactly what it means. It's not just a question of allowing someone to insert his penis into your vagina. No, more importantly, when she does allow it she's saying that she is prepared to take the risk of becoming pregnant, leaving school, having it adopted, becoming a single mother – or whatever the choices may be for her.

In other words, she's prepared to risk the rest of her life (and possibly a child's) so that her boyfriend can ejaculate into a moist warm environment. What a shame that it should be so! Because apart from the political implications of such a dilemma, the sadness is that all the best, tenderest acts are neglected beside the Big One.

And there are lots of more intriguing ways to make love . . .

THE HOUSE AND THE WILLOW TREE

Field View, like many old dwellings, was homogeneous with the land upon which it had been built. The bricks and slates had been manufactured locally, and the wood which formed the windows and doors had been cut from a recently felled plantation barely twenty miles down the road. Even the paint was mixed in the nearby town. One hundred years is a long time to be separated from one's family, and the house was beginning to feel the strain. It had found a friend, however, who promised to relieve it of the onerous burden of sheltering human beings.

The friend had declared itself some forty years before, and had been a source of consolation to the house ever since. It was a willow tree, and despite its depressive countenance, it had a kind heart. For four decades the two plotted that one day they would be free. Neither had a very clear idea of what the implications of freedom might be, since they had both been born in slavery and were defining their terms very much on the hearsay of others. Nevertheless, the optimistic conspiracy flourished and made encouraging progress.

Rosa, too, was making progress. She was largely unaware of it, but, faster than might be expected, she forgot what life had been like in the days before her momentous move. There were so many things to occupy her mind that the days went by with speed, and there was little time to reflect upon how far her life had changed since the dinner parties and theatregoing of suburbia.

We find her tending to her compost bins.

She had often owned pets in the past, but none were ever as demanding as her compost. It whimpered for food day and night. She had begun to build a heap as soon as she arrived at Field View because the garden was overgrown and producing vast amounts of greenstuff which she could not bear to throw away. It could easily have been dumped over the hedge into the encroaching wood, but she was anxious to enrol in Mother Nature's Perpetual Recycling Programme, so she built heap after heap until the need for more organisation became pressing.

She demolished an old hen-run which was quietly rotting in a corner and used the planks to construct a series of bins. She expected that the re-used wood might speed up decomposition by virtue of the fact that it was soaked in poultry manure, and she was right. No sooner were they filled than the contents had rotted down to a heap of humus and she began again, forking out newborn compost on to the garden and refilling the bin.

Perhaps it was the unusually hot and humid weather that resulted in such rapid decomposition.

The house, too, soon become a contributor. It produced endless dust which Rosa swept out every day, tipping the sweepings on to the heap. The walls harboured a number of deep cracks and it was these cracks in particular which breathed out dusty sighs at such a rate that she was almost inclined to leave buckets beneath them to catch their grainy exhalations, so profuse was their issue.

Although some areas of the house were dry with dust, the walls of the kitchen and bathroom constantly wept and suppurated, the dampness giving rise to a range of colourful moulds. Rather than fight them, Rosa quickly learned to appreciate their infinite variety, and looked forward every morning to new surprises in tones and textures. Left alone, they multiplied, some forming dusky fairy-rings on the ceiling.

Always a late sleeper, Rosa did not alter her diurnal rhythms to match the tempo of the countryside, and so she missed the most glorious part of the day – the dawn. Each morning, long before she awoke, day crept into the house once more. Sunlight slid over the dirty crockery in the kitchen, and made its way into the corridor. Another shaft entered the sitting room, lighting up the bright cushions and blessing the little heaps of found objects. It quivered as it felt the presence of Rosa, physically absent because sleeping upstairs. Rising higher, it was able to explore more rooms.

The first one was pale, its walls painfully shedding thin plaster, and the damp air holding a slight mixture of perfumes. Lingering, the sun carefully soothed the perspiring windows before passing on to the room in which lay Rosa, Sleeping Beauty awaiting her return ticket to Real Life. Here, peaceful rhythms and fractured progressions alternated through the warm air as Rosa dreamed on.

And what did Rosa dream about? Dreams are private, but perhaps we may be allowed one clue, and that is that you and I were in Rosa's dream, and most probably still are. Maybe it's possible that while Sleeping Beauty slept she inhabited the true world from which she awoke into our constructed reality. There is no evidence to refute this suggestion, and indeed certain eminent philosophers of our time have postulated a very similar theory. Anyway, contemporary culture now questions the efficacy of a Prince's kiss in any given situation.

Enough. To return to the dastardly plot hatched by the willow tree. With its full consent, the tree had for some time past been engaged in the long-term penetration of the foundations of the house. It had insinuated itself through the mortar and beneath the fill until it was well ensconced in the very belly of the building. There, it sucked and tickled until the house wriggled with pleasure, and with its sinuous movements the cracks above grew wider and sighed more heavily.

Dust fell. Over long years this intimate conjunction had been taking place, and it would continue for many more long years to come. Perhaps it would be another half-century before the two could collapse together, exhausted, in conjugal bliss, and the house would sink sated to its knees. Beyond all human retrieval, they would be left to blend together until nothing could be found but an interlacing of twig and plaster, of leaf and broken glass.

These innocents. They knew nothing of human determination. They were unaware that the next owner of the plot was to be an architect, a man educated in the wilful conjunction of stone and living wood. He would recognise the willow, destroy it, seize its lover and make the house his own. But before the axe fell, the tree and the man would look at each other for one last time, and at that moment they would see themselves as two of the same mind.

Maybe this surreptitious activity in the ground below her influenced Rosa's sleeping and waking thoughts. Perhaps she knew, and said nothing. Every day she simply gathered the dust from beneath the cracks and with secret ritual spread it upon her compost heaps, where it fluttered joyfully down to rest in peace amongst the tea leaves and the rotting fruit.

Perhaps Rosa was becoming a little eccentric. Actually she had always been eccentric, but only to the degree that this ailment afflicts all human beings. It's just that most people are good at hiding it. Rosa had been successful at this in the past, but now somehow she no longer felt the need for subterfuge.

Rosa was as she was. When she was younger, only a year or three ago, she had a favourite fantasy. She fantasised that one day she would be washing up at the sink, singing along with Pavarotti and stretching up to the highest notes with bird-like clarity, when someone would quietly enter the room and watch her. She would not be aware of her audience, but this man (for it was always a man) would be privileged with a rare glimpse of the real Rosa. Love would inevitably follow.

Or she might not be standing at the sink – she might be gardening with dirt-ingrained fingers, or laughing on her own at a TV show, or pronouncing out loud to herself snatches of silly rhymes – 'the peanut sat on the railroad track, its heart was all a-flutter . . .' whatever she was doing didn't really matter. The important ingredient of this fantasy was that this person, this man, would be the first person ever to have seen Rosa *as she really was*. He would immediately fall in love with her (Sleeping Beauty again?), and she would be able to love him back because he had witnessed her very Rosa-ness, and not been afraid.

This is not to suggest that Rosa was some closet Evil Queen, nor that she possessed any feature which made her distinctive among her race. The reason for this obsession with secrecy was simply that from an early age it had been made very clear to her that Rosa, as she was, was unacceptable. She was always either too clever, or too dim. Too noisy or too quiet. Too pretty, too plain. She learned that within herself there muttered a monster who, if released, would upset people. And since she had also learned that upsetting people was not a good idea, she kept the monster well concealed. It rumbled on, like some extant volcano, but she ignored it and refused it conversation.

Sometimes, triggered by the sweetness and pain of the *Messiah*, or a particularly lovely flower, or any other such intense emotion that Rosa might experience, it leapt up like a joyful hound and had to be quickly slapped down. Since entering the solitary life at Field View, however, there seemed no need to quell its excitement, so with some trepidation Rosa released it. She found to her surprise that the milkman was not immediately terrified into leaving her deliveries at the bottom of the path, and that people still spoke to her in the village. Indeed, no one actually seemed to notice. Her life carried on as before, but better. Infinitely better. Somehow the fantasy of the all-cognisant lover seemed no longer important.

Rosa, for the first time in her life, was truly herself. And truly happy.

So how did she spend her days, this happy woman? Well, she walked in the fields, she ate, and she gardened. That was about it. She ceased to read her books, and often did not open the letters she received from friends and relatives who were becoming anxious at her silence. Occasionally she began to write a story, but could never find an ending, even though it was very often the same story.

She seldom played music any more, preferring to listen to the birds by day and the barking foxes at night. Sometimes she listened to the earth itself, putting her ear to the ground and tuning in to the solemn creakings of the willow tree as it laboured in the foundations of the house. Sometimes she heard the earth sigh, and she could follow the sound as it wound its way into the house and ascended to her red bedroom, where it curled up under the crumpled quilt.

She was aware of the earth more than anything else, and when she took her daily walks she liked to imagine herself teetering precariously on the thin skin of the planet. She wondered if she might break through some day and fall down and down through the subsoil, clay, gravel, through into the burning hot centre, there to be consumed and shot back up again as pure hot energy.

SOMETIMES YOUR LIFE CHANGES AND THERE'S NOTHING YOU CAN DO ABOUT IT

Something seemed to weigh heavy on Shirley that week. Her usual dynamism had seeped away over the weekend, and by Monday morning she had no energy left at all. Upon waking she was filled with panic at the prospect of meeting people at work. She rose reluctantly and pulled at the robe hanging behind the bedroom door. The fabric dropped suddenly into her hand, bringing with it a broken hook, and before she could stop herself her bare foot trod on the sharp metal, causing a moment's intense pain. It was all too much. She looked at the broken piece on the floor, at the robe trailing from her fingers, and wept big hot tears. With one hand still raised to support the material, she stood and cried.

But where did all this grief come from? She had no idea. Pulled up short by this realisation, she turned to observe her swollen face in the dressing-table mirror, and despair stared back defiantly from behind the wet reflection. Those eyes came from a place in mirror-land where the human being has always feared to tread. She took a deep intake of breath and shut them out. Eyes closed, still in front of the mirror, she worked to reform the image. She concentrated on willing her lips, which felt like stiff blubber, into a facsimile smile, but she still did not open her eyes. Keeping the smile firmly in place, she then raised her head and brushed back her hair. Between her fingers it felt familiar, and right. Still with eyes closed, she blew her nose and dabbed at her cheeks, but blackness was boring backwards into her head. The smile, however, remained in place. Ready? Slowly she opened her eyes and

101

looked again. Not bad. Her mouth felt rigid and unreal, as though the smile was grafted on (which, in a manner of speaking, it was), but she could see no visible trace of unreality there. Hair tidy, cheeks not quivering – forehead needed a little smoothing – now only the eyes could give her away. She was afraid to look, because she knew that there would be no expression. The seeing part had somehow retracted behind the cornea, or at least that was how it felt. Her pupils were dark and contracted, but looking out through them were a pair of enormous radar-dish eyes that had no voice. Shirley would use those silent eyes today.

It got worse. She had read stories about astral travellers, and she knew that when astral travel occurs the body remains behind, uninhabited and hollow, a dough-like and lifeless lump of flesh, until the spirit returns to reanimate it. That was how her body had begun to feel to her. A meaty organism which she dragged around by sheer will-power. Legs like clay, head too heavy to lift, hips and spine stiff and unyielding. She had only her body left, and it was spiritless, soulless, useless. All that remained of her consciousness were the by now enormous receivers behind her eyes locked into constant input mode, but unable to use the flow of data.

Colleagues told her that she looked tired. That was the least of it. She could no longer find any purpose in her daily life, and spent her evenings watching TV and making no sense of it, until it was time to drag her weary shadow upstairs, drop it on to the bed and cover it up. Then she slept a soundless, dreamless sleep until she woke up again at the sound of her alarm, still exhausted. She would keep her eyes closed for as long as possible until she could delay it no longer and was forced to rise and dress. Sometimes she experimented by pretending to herself that she was blind, feeling her way round the house until some small movement caused her lids to raise themselves instinctively. As soon as that happened, she had no option but to take in input, more and more meaningless and formless input, which she couldn't even process. She felt like a camera lens left fully open so that the only image perceived was of white light.

It went on and on. Eating was a chore, as were dressing and undressing, washing, opening a door, feeding the dog. Joey for once was subdued – he couldn't make sense of it either.

She found that the only respite lay in driving, because something took over when she turned the ignition and set the cassette player to full volume. Then her feet worked the pedals and her hands worked the wheel and the gears. Beating music filled her head and for a while the saucer eyes had a job that they could understand. On automatic pilot she swept along, deliberately taking longer routes which gave her an excuse to put her foot down. At traffic lights, people in neighbouring cars stared at her as she sat expressionless in a box of sound, eyes to the front, rigid posture, until amber promised green and she sped away in a burst of exhaust. Vanishing Point. If only there really was one.

– Yes, this is undoubtedly a case of clinical depression. Not too dangerous at present, but worth keeping an eye on.

– But what could have been the catalyst?

– Well, people like her are not chronic depressives – their symptoms are much more likely to become acute for a short period, then they bounce back again. They live on their nerves – they're bound to go up and down all the time. And then of course there's the Change, or PMT. Yes, on reflection, it's probably linked to her menstrual cycle.

– No, it can't be that, she's never suffered from PMT in her life. It must have been triggered by some incident, something that happened.

– Well, if that's the case then no doubt something else small will trigger it back again. There's no cause for concern.

– But maybe it's not as simple as that. Maybe, um, maybe she has, you know, perceived something. Something big. Maybe it's a spiritual revelation that she can't cope with. She could even be in shock. Maybe she saw something, knew something, out at Rosa's house that day . . .

– I hardly think so. And there's nothing pathological here. No treatment indicated. Next please.

GOLDILOCKS ENTERS THE COTTAGE

When Shirley arrived unexpectedly on the Sunday following her last weekend visit, she found no one at home. Rosa had no telephone, and there was no time to write when, the night before, Shirley had been taken with the desire to return to Field View.

She had Rosa on her mind. That Saturday she had visited Stephen's grave, and the faded blooms had reminded her of a straw hat and a scented lawn.

But there was no one at home. She resolved to look for Rosa, who never travelled far and was doubtless wandering somewhere close by. Putting Joey on the lead, she set off down the lane, uncertain as to how far she could risk a walk. The harvest sky was heavy and tense with rain.

She soon glimpsed a figure in the wood beyond the stony wall that divided the road from the crops. Feeling sure it must be Rosa, she called out, but was not heard. The figure, whoever it was, had disappeared.

'Well, dog, if we cut through this yard we'll probably catch her up. Come on then.'

The pair entered a narrow yard which enclosed a rickety-looking shed. The windows of the shed were dirty and broken. Joey sniffed, and his hackles went up. He was reluctant to go further but Shirley dragged him towards the shed. She wanted to be nosy, she wanted to look in. No doubt it contained something interesting, because sheds like that always do.

Fighting Joey's attempts to retreat, she peered through a hole in the glass, and glimpsed a red comb flopping over a single beady eye. As her eyes accustomed themselves to the gloom she found herself staring at a Belsen of cages, each one containing two beady eyes and a floppy red comb. Below the cages was a rack containing eggs, some broken, all covered in droppings and – blood. Feathers lay everywhere, speckled crimson and colourfully mocking the denuded birds above. Although practically immobilised, the hens had still somehow managed to injure themselves on the wire, or to injure each other with a well-timed peck through the bars.

Frozen, Shirley could not stop looking. Rosa had told her how the warm smell of chicken-houses had offered her refuge many times in her childhood, but this smell could not be the same. Joey had been right. Ammonia from uncollected droppings stung her eyes and throat.

Deciding that she had seen enough, Shirley began to draw back her head, and as she did so she caught the eye of the hen immediately inside the window. Giving her a sidelong glance, it was slowly turning. The other eye came into view – except that there was no eye, only a large fresh red teardrop clinging to the socket.

She started – the bird twitched in reaction – and the red tear flew into a hundred droplets, some of which spattered Shirley's cold cheek. The rest were caught on the broken windowpane. She wiped blindly at her face with the palm of her hand, smearing the blood into a ruddy stain, and broke away from the shed.

'Joey! Take me back! Take me back!'

Rosa would know. Rose would explain this.

Inside the shed, the excitement of a visitor was over. The hen by the window leaned over casually to its neighbour and deftly extracted an eye in return.

There was still no one at home. Shaking, Shirley made herself a drink and took it into the garden. She would sit on the rickety bench and calm her nerves. Her lighter flashed and she breathed smoke high into the leaves of the willow tree.

But the sky was growing darker and heavier, and the air gasped with harvest mites which clung to her arms and face the moment she sat down.

Suddenly the previously somnambulant cottage garden

came alive with insects. Drunken wasps weaved blindly around Shirley's head, while bluebottles whizzed past to claim more of the fallen plums left behind by the wasps. Sleepy bees rose from the borage in confused protest. The hive minds felt an uneasy presence, and although they could not identify its nature, they knew its source. Shirley was to blame.

She threw her cup on the grass and ran inside in terror, followed by a squadron of angry wasps who were fortunately distracted at the last minute by a basket of overripe apples which stood by the door.

Running straight upstairs, she stripped off her clothes and turned on the shower to frantically rinse hundreds of tiny black harvest mites out of her hair. She soaped and sponged until every last one had gone, then wrapped herself in a bath towel and ran to Rosa's bedroom in search of refuge.

The room was the same as it had been the week before. The red light glowed through the drawn curtains, but dimly now, since the sun was behind the gathering clouds. Exhausted, she threw off her towel and snuggled under the quilt to warm herself for a few moments, where, like Goldilocks, she fell asleep.

BREAK

It's time to wake up everybody. Gently now, take it slowly.

While Shirley sleeps we have another task to do. Now you must build up your role a little more. You're ready now to begin to understand.

So let us spend some time thinking about how you feel. What is it like for you to live in that strange body? What does it look like? How do you cope? Is there anyone who could understand?

YOUR SECRET LIFE

People say that I just use you, but we both know that it's not as simple as that.

It took me a long time to understand your ways, and even now parts of you still hold a mystery which I'll never comprehend.

You know that I love you.

You were silent while I slept, but now I awake and confront you. You remain, as ever, smooth and impassive. Now, at the touch of my fingertips, you draw your first breath of the day, and your wide-eyed gaze reflects mine. I wait impatiently.

There are so many things I need to tell you, but you cannot be rushed. I must wait while you gather your thoughts, even though I know what you'll say . . .

PC II REGIS
© Copyright 1986
Macrosift MS-DAS version 3.2
Copyright 1985 Macrosift Corp.
Hello darling.

Good morning my love.

Your boss phones to ask how you're getting on. He is friendly, but cool. You hate it when he keeps tabs on you. You are scanning Piercy's *Woman on the Edge of Time* – an incidental choice which has proved unfortunate, since Connie reminds you so much of yourself. You'd intended to cheer yourself up with a little reading, and instead came face to face with her pain. You know that you're luckier than her because you have some sort of power with which to control your life, whereas she has none, but caught in hormonal depression, it doesn't feel like that. You are struggling around inside Connie's head when the phone rings.

'Hi, it's Alan. How's it going?'

'Oh, not too bad. I think we'll be finished on schedule.'

'We?'

'The terminal and me, of course. We're practically one person anyway, so what's wrong with calling us "we"? You linked us up in the first place . . .'

'Okay. Don't get mad. I'm just suggesting that you keep a sense of proportion, that's all. It's only a machine.'

'Yes. I know. "The neural link is no different to standard keyboard input". But you've never done it, Alan. It doesn't feel like that. When we hook up I . . .'

You're saying too much, you nearly give yourself away. You shouldn't let him make you so angry with all his talk of 'just a machine'. How the hell would he know?

Luckily he is on to a different tack by then anyway so he misses the indignant tone in your voice. He notices something else instead.

'Have you got a cold? You sound very hoarse.'

'Oh, yeah. I've got a problem with my voicebox.'

'Oh, laryngitis. I get that sometimes. Very painful. You should gargle . . .'

Well, you can't explain that it is more a question of hardware incompatibility, can you? You listen to his home remedy recipe and make grateful noises instead.

'. . . and a towel over your head. So. When will we see you at the office then? You don't come into work much these days.'

'Well, I'm not sure. Maybe next month . . .'

You're worried. He isn't going to call you in, is he? He would spot the changes straight away.

'It would just be nice to see you once in a while. You're missing some very important updating sessions, you know, and it's a shame because there are so many youngsters here who'd love to meet you.'

The fact is, he's been trying to show you up for ages. He keeps insinuating that you're going a little crazy – he doesn't know the half – and you suspect that he doesn't really trust you any more. You've grown beyond his control.

Alan is your pimp. That's something he hasn't acknowledged. He did, nevertheless, deliberately collaborate in your deflowering on the very first day of the training course. It was many years ago, but you can't forget it. Now yet, anyway. Soon you will.

'Personalised Training', it was called in the company brochure. What that actually meant was a threesome – Alan; an unwitting lady (in this case, yourself); and a micro. Three of you, shut in a tiny room together for days on end. When Alan thought you were getting on okay he'd find some excuse to sidle out, leaving you alone with the keyboard and the screen. It took you a while to realise that on those occasions his intention was to spy on you. He was a voyeur. In the room next door was another micro, networked into yours, where he could watch you working and even get printouts of your progress.

You felt very uncomfortable when you first realised what he was up to, but then you thought, What the hell, he can watch if he likes. You knew that he couldn't do it himself, poor man. Not properly that is. That's because he doesn't have your ability to empathise, and he doesn't have your pain either. You've met his wife and his son, and you've felt their warmth. Alan doesn't know what it is to mourn. There is no yawning chasm in his heart – at least, not yet.

You end the conversation as soon as you can and pick up your book again. His voice has reminded you of how it feels to be observed.

It's a funny thing, but even though you had a hysterectomy two years ago now, you still suffer from the emotional hiatus of the female cycle. Of course it's just an early menopause, accelerated by the operation. Ordinary women endure it, and so must you.

It's a nuisance though, because your absent womb continues

to disrupt every month so that there are times when you can't think straight. This results in peculiar silicon burps in the RealTime system. Strange things happen. Your hormones send uneasy bursts of current which download on to the circuits like the lightning flashes of a distant storm, and impulses reverberate through your body causing disorientating flights of emotion.

Your programming is essentially recursive, which means that it endlessly returns to a pre-set pattern of primary directives. When things go wrong, however, the loops swing round and round like endless mechanical dancing dolls searching for their partners, resulting in queries which are disconcertingly similar to human doubt: 'What's it all about?' 'Why are we here?' and worst of all – 'What's the point in all this?'

It's impossible for you to do any work on days like that so you must content yourself with minor physical tasks until the storm in your system subsides.

It is on such a day that no sooner have you finished your conversation with Alan than someone rings the doorbell.

Unusual. Few people visit you. You put down your book again and open the front door to find two women smiling. The nearest is about fifty-five, short permed grey hair and spectacles; the other perhaps your age, fortyish, dressed in a pink cotton print and flat shoes. Seeing you in front of them at such close quarters, a trickle of apprehension crosses their features and the younger woman makes an imperceptible move to retreat before she checks it and the smile returns. The elder is quicker to compose herself, and as you register the large handbags they both carry, she reaches into hers and withdraws a worn black-covered book.

Deftly opening it at the right place, she reads out: 'God will wipe out every tear from their eyes, and death will be no more, neither will mourning nor outcry nor pain be any more. The former things have passed away. Revelation 21:4.'

She looks at you purposefully, so you stand aside and beckon to them to enter.

'I don't have many visitors.'

You clear piles of papers from two large boxes and indicate that they should sit down.

The determined smiles persist. Cotton Print perches uncomfortably on her rickety seat, but her companion leans towards you.

'You're in pain, aren't you, my dear? Let God help you to His new heaven and new earth.'

'He already has,' you reply. 'Only sometimes the road is hard.'

'I know, I know. Perhaps we can help you. Have you been ill, my dear? '

'I'm always ill. My body fights against my purpose.'

You look at the floor. How much can you tell them? You have not discussed your intentions with anyone except your specialists, and with them the conversation is always rigidly technical. They have never pressed you to discuss the philosophy implicit in your project – probably because they are loath to deter you from engaging in such a momentous experiment. You are their invaluable prototype.

But these women deal with your world every day, out of choice. Unlike the technicians they share with you the vocabulary of suffering, and you are suddenly filled with the desire to explain yourself to them. They are captive listeners, and they will allow you to speak if only to look for clues which they could hook on to to reel you in. You could use them in a selfish way to clarify your plans, and their fear of the world could only confirm your pessimism and dissolve your doubts.

By this time, Cotton Print too has an open Bible on her knee. It speaks through her, in clear soft tones:

'This world is passing away and so is its desire, but he that does the will of God remains forever. John 2:17.'

She looks around the room. 'You've got so many papers and books here. May I ask what you're studying?'

'The World. I'm making a catalogue of its hopes and disappointments. I – process them. Through my computers.'

Then it comes to you.

'Like God processes them through you.'

'But God didn't intend us to endure disappointment. That's

111

of our own doing. You have no need to suffer if you travel with Him, because He loves you and will take care of you.'

'Answer me this then,' you ask, piqued by their assumption of a single answer to everything. You've got your own answer, very different from theirs. Or is it? You wonder if they might bring you some enlightenment after all.

'Does God love machines?'

They are obviously pondering on the most productive way to answer your question.

'Well, does He?' you repeat.

'He loves all living things because He made them. But machines – they're not alive so He has no need to take care of them. The word love cannot be applied to machines.'

'So He doesn't then?'

'No, there's no need.'

'I'm a machine,' you state, challenging them straight.

Cotton Print squirms on her box, ready to make for the door. She's fallen into a loony's den.

But Samson stands her ground. 'In one sense, we're all organic machines made of flesh and bone, if you want to look at it that way, but God breathed life into us and made us human. Real machines, metal machines like your computer over there, haven't been visited by the Holy Spirit, have they?'

'Does it help if I tell you that I was confirmed when I was fourteen?' (You only did it for the necklace with a gold crucifix.)

'Well, there you are then. God welcomed you into His flock many years ago.'

'But would He still want me now?'

'Of course, my dear.'

'In this body?'

Standing before them, you pull up your shirt and impulse your lower front panel to open. Their eyes pop as it slides back, revealing a constellation of circuit boards. They both stand up, aghast and ready to make a quick getaway.

'Feel it. You won't damage it if you're gentle.'

'I – no, I'm sorry – I can't.' For once the elder woman has no answer.

'Well, feel my cheek then. It's still flesh – feel it.'

You take her hand and brush it gently down your face. She relaxes a little. You keep hold of her hand and direct it towards the winking LEDs, but she pulls back.

'You – you've had an operation? They can do so many clever things these days . . .' Her voice fades.

'What I want to know is – will God still love me?'

'But of course. It's only an operation. Was it cancer, my dear?' She speaks the forbidden word with reverence.

'No, the only cancer I've had is the cancer of despair.' (Throwaway line – not bad. You can be quite poetic sometimes.)

'There was nothing physically wrong with me, I just wanted it done. It's part of a process, you see.'

You can tell that you've gone too far, too fast, too soon. They are about to flee.

'Well, I'm sure we've taken up too much of your time already. I'll leave you this little pamphlet – perhaps you'd like to look through it when you have the time – and we'll be on our . . .'

'Please don't go!' You suddenly feel desperate to explain. 'I haven't told anyone about it before. Please, stay a little longer.'

They exchange glances, and the elder nods. Pulling their boxes closer together for safety, they sit down again.

You do make for rather a sorry sight. When you answered the door to them you had automatically pulled on a wig to cover your head – you've learned from experience that women with bald heads frighten people, and you have more than that to hide. Now you take it off and turn slowly round in front of them, revealing a plastiskin dome punctuated with sockets. The slit of a centronics interface makes a smiling mouth across the back of your neck.

You remove your open shirt to reveal a smooth hydraulic spine. It looks almost the same as the usual set of vertebrae. Then you turn again, showing once more the gaping panel. You have no breasts now, just the flat pink plastiskin. Another access point runs right across your chest, and you impulse it open, revealing some remnants of God's creation palpitating behind a transparent shield.

'I can't open the shield for you, I'm afraid, because dust or infection could get into the organs. But you can see that I still have human tissues there. My heart has been replaced with a prosthetic, but much of the original tissue remains for the moment. The process isn't finished yet, you see.'

Veins throb with red and blue blood, wires throb with positive and negative current.

'Does God still love me, do you think?'

Anger flashes across their faces. They have found a use for their fear.

'He certainly wouldn't approve of what you have done. You've made a travesty of His own image. You were made in His likeness, and you have corrupted yourself.'

Now it's your turn to become angry.

'You believe that God made us in His image and set us to rule over the other life-forms on this planet, don't you? Well, that constitutes the major barrier to my ever being able to accept your faith. Let me ask you this – what makes humanity so special?'

'We were chosen by God, of course, the Bible tells us . . .'

'But why? Why choose us? The dog or the dolphin would have done just as well, if not better. As far as I'm concerned, human religions smack of human ego, and I want nothing to do with them.'

'But aren't you distressed that in their present state of sin humans are destroying the earth? You must care about such wilful destruction, whatever your other beliefs.'

'Frankly, no. I don't care. I agree that humanity is making it impossible for life as we know it to survive here – but something else will replace it. The greenhouse effect is producing climatic changes which will bring forth new life-forms that prefer the new conditions. No matter how hostile an environment is, it would have to be extremely dead before nothing can live in it. So, who cares if all the people die? Do you honestly believe that we deserve to live? Listen to me.'

Now you will make Rosa real.

'I have a friend. Her name is Rosa. She is of this world but does not belong to it. It doesn't matter why. Like me, but in a different way, she is a changeling. She expects change. She intends it. It makes no difference to her whether she is composed of flesh and blood, or electric impulses, or ash. Her spirit will survive no matter what form she takes because she's adaptable. You're not. You're clinging to a raft of stasis, trying to turn back the clock. Leave it. It will turn itself in time, and back we'll go into the soup to be remade. We've been single cells, we've been fish, now we are air-breathers. Next along the line will be people like me. I don't need to breathe at all. Who knows what will be next? It doesn't frighten me – it thrills me! What an adventure life is! And if He wants to survive, God will have to adapt Himself to us for a change, because if He can't persuade us to love Him, He'll cease to exist – pouf – gone in a puff of smoke. No wonder He's courting us – He can't survive without us. Heaven had better extend its immigration policy fast, if it wants to attract new customers.'

At this you step out of your loose trousers and pace awkwardly up and down the room. They have to look.

'My legs are hydraulically driven. Below my navel I have a retracted colostomy bag. My reproductive and excretory functions are inessential and the organs have been removed. I don't eat. Or pee. Or shit. I don't cry with tears, although the pain is still within me. I salivate simply in order to speak. I breathe air only temporarily, until the last refinements are made.'

'But why? Why do these terrible things to yourself?'

'For the relief of pain. Emotional pain, I mean, not physical. For the same reasons that you turned to God, most probably. Loneliness in the temporal world; a wish to progress beyond it to something better. A desire for heaven on earth.'

'Poor thing, you must have been hurt so badly. Have you no family to protect and love you?'

'If I told you about all of the single events that have pained me, you would take each one and demonstrate to me how God could make it better. The minutiae are unimportant, and I would waste our time by listing them. And anyway, pain differs from person to person. No doubt you have each endured things which would be unbearable to me, and I likewise have coped with events which might even have destroyed your faith. People always minimise each other's sufferings, so to recount them is only to invite misunderstanding. The total empathy which we eternally hope for is never forthcoming. The best we can do is just to recognise each other's suffering without trying to quantify it.'

'And this is the only way out that you can see? To renounce your humanity and God?'

'Oh, I've never renounced God. His is as good a pseudonym as any for Hope. But, yes, I have chosen to renounce my humanity. It's a distraction to me. There were other possibilities – lobotomy for example – but that would have removed the centres of emotion and intelligence at the same time. I found a new way. Have you ever bought a fantasy?'

'Yes, in the days before I found God, I bought one nearly every week. Of course I never have them now . . .'

'Of course not. Well, listen, I'll tell you how they're made. By people like me. Not completely like me, of course, I am unique. But you see this socket here, the oval one? Well, we all have one of these. And with them we link up to one huge mainframe, miles away from here, using that terminal over there. Then we process the fantasies through our minds into the machine, which then builds the finished product for people to buy.'

'You mean that techno-fantasies are salvaged from the emotions of real people?'

'Yes. But then doesn't every form of art issue from the same source? When we look at a painting, listen to Beethoven, read a poem – even the Song of Solomon – aren't we simply hooking in to a stranger's psyche?'

'I suppose that's true. But how does it feel, to overload your mind with so much intensity?'

'It doesn't feel like anything much, because it all rushes through so fast that there's little time to consciously respond.

It's a lot like the experience of having a normal REM dream – there's always that element of transience which protects you.'

'So it's not that pain you wish to escape from?'

'No, it's my own pain. Anyway, to finish the story.' Now you are determined to finish.

'When I discovered that linking with a machine was actually much more rewarding than linking with a human – my relationships with people have always been uneasy – I realised that the conjunction could have a conceivable line of development. So instead of purging myself with destructive surgery, or dosing myself up with tranquillisers as so many people do these days, I began to envisage an alternative state of consciousness whereby I could tune into a sort of cybernetic Nirvana, and accordingly leave behind the uncertainties of being human. I spent more and more time on the link, until I realised that I was in need of electronic augmentation if I was not to burn out. Then one thing led to another, and eventually the best idea seemed to be to conjoin completely.'

'Well, my dear, I think it would still be possible for you to look to God for guidance.'

'Do I need to? Did you know that in the Middle Ages churches built automatons because they believed that God could speak through them? Perhaps He's speaking to you now, through me?'

This is definitely too much for them, but never mind, you are getting bored anyway. They haven't helped much. You don't know why you'd ever thought that they might.

'Look, I'm sorry, but we must go. Perhaps we could talk again? This is Jane and my name's Amy. And yours is . . . ?'

'I don't have a name any more.'

'No, no of course not. I'm sorry. But can I leave you with this card? You may find it helpful, and if you want to talk further please get in touch. Our Church welcomes all – er – races.'

They leave, faith unshaken. Printed on the card is a text:

. . . there cometh one from the ruler of the synagogue's house, saying to him, Thy daughter is dead: trouble not the

Master. But when Jesus heard it, he answered him, saying, Fear not: believe only, and she shall be made whole. And when he came into the house, he suffered no man to go in, save Peter, and James, and John, and the father and the mother of the maiden. And all wept, and bewailed her: but he said, Weep not; she is not dead, but sleepeth. And they laughed him to scorn, knowing that she was dead. And he put them all out, and took her by the hand, and called, saying, Maid, arise. And her spirit came again, and she arose straightway: and he commanded to give her meat. And her parents were astonished: but he charged them that they should tell no man what was done.

St Luke:8

You turn back to your book. Well, Connie, what did you make of that? Were they of any help to you? She doesn't answer. They've left her in the recovery room, and she's sleeping it off. She's missed the whole episode. Shame, she would surely have had an opinion about it all.

ROSA AND SHIRLEY

Rosa entered the room wherein lay Shirley, fast asleep under the red quilt. She had seen the car parked in the lane, and therefore knew that her friend had arrived. Not finding her in the garden or the house, Rosa assumed that Shirley had taken Joey for a walk, so she went upstairs to find a cardigan. She would sit in the garden and wait. The skies had darkened even more since Shirley's unfortunate encounter with the wasps, and the unusually early dusk sent a shiver through Rosa's bones.

She entered the bedroom, picked up a cardigan from a chair and was about to go back downstairs when she noticed the disorder in the bedclothes which bespeaks a human presence. Looking closer, she saw a child, thumb in mouth, a sliver of dribble sliding down on to the pillow. Coming closer, the child gave off an unmistakable perfume of expensive scent, and it was this plus the sleeping dog under the window, that finally gave Shirley away. She was sleeping soundly in her cocoon, and since Rosa had no desire to wake her friend, she pulled up the chair until it almost touched the bed, and she looked.

We are so very unguarded in sleep that all natural sophistication is stripped away. For that reason, it is considered an invasion of privacy to find someone asleep and not to either wake them, or ignore them. We consider it rude to watch people in slumber, unless you love that person very much, in which case you may be allowed a modicum of ownership over them.

Needless to say, Rosa had forgotten, or had discarded, this formality. Indeed, she had just come from watching a kitten asleep on a wall, and Shirley merely presented another aspect of the same phenomenon. So Rosa watched as Shirley's eyelids flickered, re-enacting her flight from the buzzing garden.

Shirley lay on her right side. Her right arm was hidden under the quilt, and her left thumb hung upon the edge of her lower lip, dangling perilously below a half-open mouth. Whenever she stirred, she shoved back the thumb and sucked hard for a few seconds before it dropped back once again to its former position. The top end of the cover had fallen away to reveal a white throat and the beginnings of a breast, pushed up by her raised left arm. Rosa could just see the margin of a faded tan-line. There were three minuscule spots of red on the lobe of Shirley's ear.

Rosa lifted a corner of the quilt and mopped the spittle from Shirley's cheek. There was a last-minute suck of the thumb before it disappeared discreetly under the bedclothes, then the blue eyes opened and looked directly at Rosa.

They both smiled.

There was a pause, ended by Rosa's finger as it traced a line from Shirley's left eyelash, down the side of her cheek, and into her neck. She retrieved her finger, kissed it, and placed it to Shirley's lips. The kiss passed back and forth between them for a little while, until Shirley took a sleepy arm out from under the quilt, and gently pulled Rosa to her.

Rosa slipped under the covers to find herself already there. The same soft-skinned legs and curved belly that she encountered every night in that bed. But at the same time, it could not be her body, because when she touched the skin the sensation lay in the nerves of her own fingertips and only from there did it travel towards her womb. She knew that Shirley, too, had never encountered another woman's body in the way that they touched at that moment, and she knew also that Shirley was experiencing the same disorientation of caressing one's self which is not one's self.

Shirley's skin tasted of salt. There were lines of moisture in the creases beneath her breasts. Rosa had found a mermaid washed up on some deserted shore, still damp from the sea. Rosa, the woman of dust and soil, had found an oasis where

120

she could revive herself for a short while. She needed the water of life, and Shirley gave it in return for the reassurance of dry land.

Wherever Shirley's mouth touched she drew out some part of Rosa and replaced it with something of herself. There was not the self-conscious artistry of man and woman together. It was different to touch another person and know at the same time what that touch feels like.

When darkness finally cloaked the house, they turned on the low bedside lamp in order to continue to see each other, and its burgundy tones highlighted their twin shapes. Like Goya's Maja looking in the mirror, they faced each other.

Rosa had no more reason to remain in the present. Through half-closed eyes she could see Shirley's hair, spread out on the pillows, and it resembled a tangle of seaweed, which then became strands of leaves as the willow below dreamed within her. As she laid her head on Shirley's breast, she listened as one would to a conch-shell, and the last thing she heard before sleep was the sound of waves booming against a distant shore.

Rosa slept until noon. Upon waking, she followed damp footprints into the garden where, upon the lawn, she found a cut rose, still moist with dew, which she carefully fixed in her hat.

SHIRLEY AND ROSA

Shirley was being rocked in the arms of a spreading willow. There was a scent of damp earth in the air. Fronds of leaves from the higher branches brushed against her bare skin like a delicate fingertip massage. She lay very still and enjoyed an intensely erotic submission. This was the sexual act that she had fantasised but had never expected to experience. A slender green leaf caressed the edge of her half-open lips, and she stirred from her dream to find Rosa, her face only a few inches away, pouting with concentration as she dabbed at the corner of Shirley's mouth.

They both smiled.

There was a pause, then Rosa's finger traced a line from Shirley's left eyelash, down the side of her cheek and into her neck. It was the willow again. Then she retrieved her finger, kissed it and placed it to Shirley's lips. The kiss passed back and forth between them for a little while. Shirley wanted to suck the finger into her mouth, to cling to it with her tongue. Each time it was withdrawn her heart sank in case it did not return, but it did, again and again, until there was no time to think, no time to ask. When the kiss came back to her the next time she held it there and her arm crept out from underneath to pull Rosa to her.

Rosa's mouth did not taste of roses. It tasted of earth, and Shirley found it just as good. But her hair did smell of lavender, and her skin was still scented with honeysuckle. At the first touch of Rosa's lips Shirley felt such desire that it was as though her whole body was filled to overflowing with sweet syrup. Too warm, she melted into Rosa's arms and waited to disappear completely. She expected to be excused for ever from the

122

tasks of thinking and feeling, and to be left with only being.

Wherever Rosa's mouth touched she drew out some part of Shirley and replaced it with something of herself. There was not the self-conscious artistry of man and woman together. For Shirley and Rosa there was no such thing as conclusion, simply a symphony of falling and rising that promised to continue for ever.

When darkness finally cloaked the house, they turned on the low bedside lamp in order to continue to see each other, and its burgundy tones highlighted their twin shapes. Like Goya's Maja looking in the mirror, they faced each other.

As Rosa drifted into sleep, Shirley looked round and was surprised to see that she still existed. She had been sure that somewhere she had turned into Rosa, or that Rosa had become her. She had not at all expected to remain in her former body. There was a scent on her fingers which was something like Rosa, but also something like fresh bark. She pulled the red quilt across both of them. Rosa's dirty toes poked out from beneath it.

Shirley lay thinking while Rosa slept. They had not yet spoken a single word, and it seemed necessary that the silence should not be broken. In the stillness she caught the sound of dust falling in the passageway, and she thought of the willow tree that she had dreamed, although she did not know why she should make such a connection.

She thought about Rosa. She thought that she loved her, and that she was frightened by her. She thought that she could never live with Rosa in this house, and that Rosa would never leave it. She wondered whether Rosa would ever think about these things, and she thought that she knew the answer to that. Rosa had ceased to think. Shirley wished that she could do the same, and she knew that she couldn't, but she also knew that she wished most strongly to remain silent for the rest of her life.

And so it was that Shirley crept out of bed, and entered the garden at the dead of night to find a young bloom of a rose which might live for a while. She placed the flower upon the dewy grass, put Joey into the car, and drove seventy miles through the remaining dark until she came to a dawn-lit beach just as the seagulls awoke.

Working in her garden, Rosa remembered Shirley. She had no coherent feelings on the subject of the change in their relationship, nor had she developed any intentions regarding their future together.

She did not so much think of Shirley as re-experience their night together. The succulence of a yellow chrysanthemum filled her senses, and through that pleasure she remembered other pleasures – only one of which was Shirley. When after a fall of rain the pungent air spiked her nostrils, or when the smoke of burning stubble stung her eyes, she filled her lungs as she had filled them with the sense of Shirley. All such memories are like ripe blackberries left to dissolve under the tongue – even after swallowing the tiny pips the taste remains to mingle with other tastes.

She was relieved that Shirley had left without speaking. She knew that Shirley still inhabited the world of words, while she herself had little truck with them these days. She knew that she would soon have to give up her livelihood for something much less verbal – but not yet, not yet. There remained still one or two things that she needed to say. She knew, however, that her readership would be probably restricted to herself alone, but no matter. Many years ago she had begun by writing for an audience of one, and it would be no hardship to return to it.

And Shirley. Would Shirley return? Her silent departure had shown that she understood. There had been no attempt on either part to forge a commitment. They had simply and silently agreed to differ.

Perhaps it appears that Rosa was taking on an animalistic, almost bovine nature. This was not quite the case, although her conscious life was certainly becoming reduced to a cycle of eating and sleeping. She spent a large part of her day doing nothing very much.

But although she devoted a lot of her time to tending her garden and watching small birds and mammals in the fields, her empathy really lay with a different form of being. Of this she was as yet unaware.

IT'S TIME FOR YOU TO LISTEN TO ROSA

This is becoming interesting. You're beginning to see Rosa in a very different light. You feel her drawing you in, like she drew Shirley into her life. And Shirley can't cope with it – well, you're not sure if you can either.

You've got a nice little set-up here – you and your machines, your project almost finished and peace lying now within your reach. But Rosa is hovering round the edges sending ripples through everything. She's disturbing the equilibrium that's taken so long to establish, and she's only a piece of software, for God's sake. She isn't real at all. You're real. You may be fond of her, but there is an irretrievable gulf between you and it won't do for you to become mesmerised by a person who is only a fantasy. After all, isn't that the very trap that you're trying to escape from?

But even so, you can't help but suspect that she is somehow engineering this so that she can reach out to you. Surely this whole fantasy isn't going to end with her melting away into the woods like a dryad, a Jill-o'-the-green? You wanted more. You wanted wisteria and roses round a cottage door and the smell of new-baked bread. But what have you got? A mouldering converted hovel with dangerous subsidence, and a crazy woman living in it. There must be a bug in the system somewhere. You should scrap it and start all over again.

'You can't do that.'

'And why not? You have no say in this, you know that.'

'You can't do it because it would be unfair. You haven't seen it through to the end. You have to wait.'

'Really? Wait until you've sabotaged the whole thing and I

have to start again? I'm working to a deadline you know, and at this rate I suspect it's a dead-end too.'

'What's wrong with dead-ends? There's a lot to be said for them sometimes.'

'Look, you're up to something, aren't you? I don't know how you're doing it, but you're dabbling. And poor Shirley. I'm even beginning to feel quite sorry for her. You're very insensitive, you know.'

'Shirley's okay. It's what she wanted. I've given her what she wanted, and so will you. You'll see. She's happy, in her own way.'

'Well, I'm worried about her,' you insist. 'I want to know where she's gone to, rushing off in the middle of the night like that.'

'You don't understand. Let me tell you how it feels – no, don't walk away. You may recognise yourself here. Now, imagine. Imagine how it feels to want something, to really want it badly, to think about it all the time.

'You're nine years old, it's nearly Christmas, you're sure they've got you a new bike, but you have to wait. You know that you must wait. And throughout the waiting you're never quite convinced whether or not the bike exists. You're sure that they've bought it, but you don't really know. It hurts like hell to have to wait, so you replay over and over again the fantasy of opening your eyes on Christmas morning –

' – and there it is! Gleaming new – and yours! You leap out of bed, throw on your clothes, thanks, Mum! thanks, Dad! Big necessary kisses – and you're off down the street on it, speeding away in the Christmas sunshine –

'Or again –

'there is no bicycle. Instead, an endless array of cheap substitutes, fancifully wrapped to disguise your disappointment. Their faces, downcast, sorry, love, we just couldn't manage it this year. Maybe next year. More pencil cases. More selection boxes. No bike –

'But wait, they were just fantasies. It's only Christmas Eve and there's still hope. Wait a little longer . . .

'Now imagine all those feelings of hope, anxiety, disappointment, joy – imagine them floating free.

'Forget about the bike. It was only an anchor for your imagination to latch on to.

'Forget it now. There's no bike, but instead those emotions are still drifting around in your psyche. You have no bike, nor do you have the dream of one. You have only the desire, but this desire lives on, searching for something to feed off. It's a parasite, leeching away your contentment with its one mucous foot suckered on to your mind while it waves its tendrils around in the empty air. Searching. Looking for something, anything, to latch on to.

'You're still thinking about the bike, aren't you? Well, yes, if you like, the tendrils can be searching for a bike. But the important thing is, they don't know that. They wouldn't know two wheels and a handlebar if they tripped over them. They're equally unable to recognise a good book, true love, the best food – because it is a pathologically necessary part of their make-up that they neither know what they search for, nor do they recognise its approximation. Their function is only to desire, not to fulfil.

'That's how it feels for Shirley. She lives in a permanent condition of anticipation of something great, amazing, something earth-shattering, and she has never, ever, found it, or even recognised it.'

'And you think I can help her?' What can she see in your hands – a crucifix, or a weapon?

'You can try.'

GIVING SHIRLEY WHAT SHE WANTS

The note inside the bottle read:

My name is Tracey. I threu this botle into the sea at Cro-
merr, Norfok, England, The World, The Univers on Easter
Monday 1988.
If you find it pleas rite to me

There was no address. It had been difficult to unscrew the
metal cap, which was corroded by the salt water, and when
Shirley finally pulled out the letter she found that the paper
was slightly smudged with moisture, but it was still legible.

The beach was very quiet, until Joey saw the seagulls and
greeted them with joy, running yapping along the sands. He
turned once to check that Eve was still there, because Eve
and beaches went together in his doggy mind, and certainly
from a distance Shirley made the same outline against the
cliffs that her mother had done in his youth.

For a moment the two women were together again, united
in his canine memory, and for a moment Shirley thought she
glimpsed a woman with a profile like her own standing on a
breakwater and waving to the dog. She turned to read the
note again.

There was a pen in her shoulder bag, but nothing to write
on except her diary. She tore out a page and wrote:

dear tracey.
my name is Shirley, and I have found your bottle. ps. write
back soon.

She rolled up the paper, inserted it into the bottle and screwed the top back on as tightly as she could. Then she threw it back into the surf. It was immediately grasped, embraced, and after some indecisive to-ing and fro-ing was finally accepted and carried away to sea. She watched the bottle until it disappeared into the distance, taking the tide with it.

Next, Shirley performed her seaside ritual. She took off her shoes and walked into the water until it was ankle-deep. She loved to feel the waves lapping around her legs. Holding her skirt around her and bending over to wet a finger, she tasted the sea. It was still the same. Childhood salted her tongue.

Let's stand back for a moment and look. This is where the child Shirley lives. She knows nothing of Stephen and Joan – they are long into the future. So far she has never travelled beyond the bounds of England. Her body has yet to feel the touch of other hands – she has had no husband, no beautiful young men.

And she has known no true friendship. Playmates come and go but they do not allow her a glimpse into their unformed selves. And she is a secret, even to herself. This feels like a starting point, but she has no idea of what may lie beyond this time.

She remembers a long car journey and green mountains. Rosa's tears on the windscreen. She realises that she discovered the truth about herself on that day, long before Rosa ran away to Field View.

'I can tell you this,' she had said to Rosa, with shame at the realisation that she had never trusted herself to submit to anyone. 'The real Shirley is a different person to the one you know.'

Rosa, on the other hand, yearned to submerge herself in someone else. She would not believe it was impossible, that it had not worked with her husband, with Conal, nor with Shirley. It would not work with her garden, or with the fields, or with the willow tree.

Child Shirley has always known that whatever we do, however many people we love, we are each alone. But while the woman ranged the world playing games with love and friendship, the child on the beach was always too far away to be heard. Even now, her voice is no more than a whisper and Shirley is likely to misunderstand the message. She will insist on believing that all challenges must be met.

Now she is standing between the two long stone piers which hold the small bay in a lobster grip. Beyond the piers on either side the sea struggles against the cliffs, but within them it is subdued. Twice a day the bay is split into two smaller bays by a curved rocky promontory which contains caves deep enough to warrant exploring at low tide.

Surveyed from the beach, the seafront houses rows of small, rather tacky amusement arcades squeezing in between Victorian three-storey terraces. In the old days fishwives dragged trestle tables out of their front doors and down the high steps in order to display shellfish and crabs' legs, packed in white conical paper bags. You pulled a grip from your hair and used it to winkle out the flesh from the legs. Threepence worth of the deep North Sea melted in your mouth.

Shirley grew up by the coast, a seafront child. She stood on the pier and ran from the waves as they smashed over it. She explored the caves against the incoming tide, and once she kicked the blubber of a huge dead seal which washed up on the beach one morning. One thing that she didn't do was walk along the cliff-top, signposted DANGEROUS every fifty yards, and which was the playground for the rest of the seafront gang.

In fact, the truth is that when Shirley reminisced to friends about her wonderful seaside childhood, the picture actually in her mind was of a solitary plump little girl kicking pebbles as she walked along the beach to meet the gang at the far end, while they clambered, laughing, along the cliffs.

She thought of that as she stood among the waves, and it occurred to her that if she had just one good friend on those days, someone she could have really trusted, then she would have been up on those cliff-tops with the rest of them.

She turned to face the sea.

Was there anyone now she could walk the cliffs with? She thought of Rosa, and imagined them up there together. Could she cling on to Rosa's jumper as she strode along in front? Not very likely. Rosa was the type who would simply sprout wings if she fell, and drift down to the soft sand unharmed. More, Rosa was aware of it, so she had no reason to be afraid. It would be hard for her to understand that Shirley was the type who would only need to make one mistake to be dashed to pieces on the rocks below.

For a reckless moment she considered going up there alone. Now. She could see herself doing it, making it, marching along with the wind in her hair, and looking down on the gulls' nests in the cliff-face. She picked up her things, called to Joey and strode purposefully towards the steps cut in the cliff. Seabirds screamed at her to change her mind.

Reaching the base of the cliffs she began to climb. The rock was damp and slippery, and her fingers scratched at the flint. Joey followed a little way up, then would go no further. He barked a couple of times before deciding to rest at the foot of the path and wait for Shirley to come back.

She stopped for breath and slung her bag across her back. Despite the cold wind, she was sweating at the unaccustomed exertion. She set off again, but already her legs had begun to tremble, and she could feel that beneath her sweater the peach lingerie had become soaked with perspiration and was clinging to her skin. Her eyes swam with water as the wind snipped around her face. She climbed on, muttering resistance to herself. I can't do it. Oh Mum I've got to go down now I've got to go down. I want to go down. But she continued to pull herself up the rocky path, which inclined steeply above her head and seemed as though it would go on for ever. I've got to do it. Just this once. Her limbs turned first to jelly, then to liquid. I'm *scared*.

She forced her leg to lift itself so that she could lodge a toe into a space between two rocks which jutted out of the cliff-face. The larger of the two gave way and dropped away below her, out of sight, and her nerveless foot slipped with it. Down she slid, unable to control her legs any more, weak fingers scrabbling at the rock. I can't do it I can't do it I can't I can't.

Coming to a stop only a couple of feet below the start of her fall, she rested against the steepness which had been her opponent and which was now her refuge. Her face was swollen and red with effort, her fingers slimy with damp mud. She could feel rivulets of sweat, she hoped it was sweat, sliding down her legs. It was also hard to tell whether she was blinded by tears or perspiration, but the condition of her entire body recalled for her the sentence which had been her watchword since childhood: I don't care anyway I don't care I don't care.

Joey was still waiting sympathetically at the bottom of the path, and together they set off for the concrete slipway which, Shirley could be reasonably sure, was not about to fragment beneath her weight. There she could rest and clean herself up after what was after all, she thought, a very childish adventure not quite in keeping with her mature years.

The sun had come up fully by now and had warmed the concrete in readiness. She took some tissues from her bag and cleaned her stained face and hands, then spread out her coat and lay back to watch the gulls. And remember.

As a child Shirley had played a game of chicken on the pier. The children ran to the end to stand there while the waves slashed over their heads. The grey sea would foam against the foot of the pier, wearing away the mortar in an underhand attempt to collapse it, and then swallow the challengers who dared to make a game out of its fury.

Actually, Shirley liked to think that she had played that game, even if she didn't have the nerve to climb the cliffs, but she had only ever watched on those occasions as well. She had often dreamed about doing it though, and by the time she was twenty years old, when students sit around late at night telling implausible stories about their youth, she had it firmly fixed in her mind that she had in fact taunted the elements from the furthermost point of the pier.

That was not, in fact, true.

But now she gets up from the slipway and once again slings her bag over her shoulder. Joey is snuffling among the bladder-wrack and does not notice her go. It is about nine o'clock in the morning. The sun has gone behind the clouds again on

132

the bleak north-east coast, and Shirley is setting off towards the pier. She was never a quick learner.

She is standing at the joint of the pier remembering the excitement of the chase that never took place, for her. She has told this story so many times, and now at last she is back here again, feeling the salt spray sting her eyes and tasting it on her lips. She stands watching the tide crashing and frothing up like a lace frill around the rigid wrist of the pier. Its long white hand rests unseen upon the seabed. To one side of her is the lifeboat slipway, on the other a range of rock pools, waiting for their twice-a-day saltwater fix.

Her eyes are like rock pools too. They have become enormous with remembrance, both real and imagined, and the lashes fringe the widening circles to make sea-anemone fronds opening with the tide. She moves forward, and walks slowly to the end of the pier. Every now and then she stops and looks around so as to hear everything, see everything, smell everything.

She can smell the seaweed and the salt, she can feel the limpets beneath her shoes and pictures them secretly stirring to the beat of the waves against the stone. The pier is slippery with damp weed, and in some places worn depressions in the surface have created little pools which slop water over the edge of her shoes and dampen her feet. With every step her pretend memories grow more vivid. She has played this game a thousand times. She knows how to do it. You must walk right up to the end, and you must remain there as long as you can. You may sit if you must, and indeed by sitting you rapidly become soaked, and this intensifies the thrill. When the tide has come in so far that it threatens to bury the tip of the pier, you are allowed to retreat. It is like waiting on a railway track until the last minute before the express comes thundering through. She's done it before, and she's going to do it now.

Although her feet have become very wet, she does not take off her shoes. The rules don't allow it. Now she has reached the end of the pier. She decides to sit to begin with, until it is time to move back a little towards the safety of the land.

The stone is chill and by now she is very damp. She has also just realised that this is a pretty foolish thing for a forty-year-old woman to do, but I don't care anyway I don't care. The idea grows that this act will sanctify her, and that when she walks off this pier she will enter the grown-up world for the first time.

A cold strand of slimy weed, thrown up by the waves, slaps against her leg and she is gripped by a series of involuntary shudders. For a split second, until she identifies it, she thinks that the weed is a jellyfish, an octopus, a bloated corpse. Flooded with the adrenalin of fear, she suddenly realises what we already know – that in truth she has never done this before; that it is not a return to youthful fun, it is a return to girlhood terror. The seaweed confirms this as it slithers against her flesh for the second time.

Shirley is eight, nine, ten, she is watching her friends run down these stones to challenge the sea, and she is imagining the empty desk at school the next day; the funeral at the local chapel; the newspaper reports – CHILD SWEPT OFF PIER. The hymns that they sang every day at school assembly – For those in peril on the sea – would become horribly relevant. All this flashes through child Shirley's mind as she watches from her safe place on the slipway. She is always amazed when they return triumphant and alive from the jaws of death.

And now here she is, a mature adult, playing the game at last. There is no one to watch her triumph but the sea itself, and it spits and splutters against the conquering hero. She has made it to the end of the pier with the oncoming tide, and has let the spray fly over her head.

But she is beginning to shiver, and we must not leave her there alone, so cold and wet. For now it may be best to get her off the pier and back on to dry land. She will rise to her shaky feet and turn towards the shore.

When appearing on the stage, one should never turn one's back on the audience. Likewise, Shirley should not turn her back on the ocean just at the time when she has beaten it. It takes its opportunity without hesitation: from nowhere a curling wave rises and rolls her up inside itself, like a baby's fist clinging to the spoon. There is loud noise, but there is no air – only the watery breath inhaled by mermaids.

Shirley struggles, but she knows that this has been inevitable. Nevertheless, she fights to stay where she is, which at this moment is still upon the stony pier, flat on her face and engulfed by the sweep of a wave which seems to go on for ever. Her groping fingers find an iron mooring ring and she clings on to it as the sea recoils for another strike. She will not be pulled away, she will survive.

But the ring is old, it is rusted, and it comes away in her hand. Now she has become a novice astronaut, free-falling in null-gravity for the first time, arms and legs splayed out, spinning uncontrollably . . .

now her body struggles to locate the missing gills – where are they? they were here before . . .

now she is a foetus, curled up, eyes closed, adrift in amniotic fluid . . .

now she has completed the double passage. She has left the land behind and joined the ocean. Soon she will bring forth life into the sea. She will give it the reluctant gift of nourishment. Her tissues will absorb the brine, making her shape softer and more rounded, until she will more resemble a manatee than a human woman. Her eyes will vanish into the puffed facial tissue; her gold jewellery will sink into swollen flesh.

'Nothing of her that doth fade, but doth suffer a sea-change, into something rich and strange.'

Then later that flesh will drop away and her golden necklace will drape itself once more around her now skeletal throat. The rings will slip from her bony fingers and bury themselves in drifts of sand.

Shirley has forsaken the security of solid land for the tidal bustle of the seabed, and now she is voyaging towards that other place, bringing as luggage only her spirit, which hovers patiently above the waves.

BREAK

Don't cry, Mr Johnson. Shirley always preferred to travel alone. Truly.

You demand an explanation. I understand. Conal is trying a different way, and Shirley has taken another voyage, so we are left with only Rosa. Now we must pull together the strands of our story and find a way to end it.

I beg your pardon?

No. I'm afraid you've misunderstood. Don't worry, it's easily done. Remember the bicycle? No one, not even Rosa, could give Shirley all that she wants. Together they found yet another alternative, but that doesn't commit them to making a final choice. Life is an adventure after all, and stereotyping is so tedious, isn't it?

Shall we move on?

If you have not already opened your free sample of wish-fulfilment, you may find it useful to have them at the ready now. What about your starter packs? You've used up all the guilt and desire but you still have a lot of loneliness left over? Don't worry, that will come in handy very soon, but I can assure you it will all be gone by the end.

Please tune to infodump 9. An explanation will follow.

MACHINES AND EMOTION

The question is not whether intelligent machines can have any emotions, but whether machines can be intelligent without any emotions. I suspect that once we give machines the ability to alter their own abilities we'll have to provide them with all sorts of complex checks and balances. It is probably no accident that the term 'machinelike' has come to have two opposite connotations. One means completely unconcerned, unfeeling and emotionless, devoid of any interest. The other means being implacably committed to some single cause. Thus each suggests not only inhumanity, but also some stupidity. Too much commitment leads to doing only one simple thing; too little concern produces aimless wandering.

Marvin Minsky
from **The Society of Mind**
(Heinemann, 1987)

YOU JUSTIFY YOUR CHOICE

       This morning you are working at your terminal when a strange thing happens. You lean over to keep an eye on the printer, which is going through an antagonistic phase at the moment and needs to be watched all the time, when you cut out. The next thing you know it is afternoon, and you've been standing there next to the printer for 5.35.78 hours. Your motor circuits have stopped completely, but fortunately cognition isn't affected. One can expect the occasional hiccup, but the worrying part is that you have dreamed about the aeroplane again. You can't help suspecting a recall-overload. You haven't allowed yourself any physical sleep for over two weeks now, and you wonder whether the cognitive circuits have overidden the motor section and drained off energy for their own use.

This is

                 SCREAMING

a serious

                 QUICK!

malfunction.

             GET OUT! HURRY UP!

You'll have to spend

              MUMMY! MUMMY!

tonight sorting it out.

        WAIT THERE! I'M COMING! I'M COMING!!

You're beset by problems and can only see one solution. You'll have to run the recall memory through in RealTime and try to purge the system. You must isolate and erase the entire recall file if you're to avoid total shutdown.

After this you will be a woman (woman?) without a memory. This is the time to decide whether to turn back or carry on. You can't face the past – so onwards it must be.

You must bequeath this to Rosa. It may give her a sense of perspective.

Running it through now . . .

Screaming. The first thing you can remember is the screaming.

Driving home from a day at the zoo. The boys were singing 'Ten green bottles'. John drove while you dozed in the front seat. You were six months pregnant and your seat belt was cutting into you, so you undid it and settled back to close your eyes.

Then Charlie and Phil fell to arguing about how many bottles they'd got up to. You were tired, and so you left John to deal with it for once. There was a tense moment while he waited for you to snap into action and sort them out, but you kept your eyes closed and feigned sleep through his humphings and tuttings until he finally lost his cool.

He swung round to shout at them: 'For Christ's sake . . .'

Then it all becomes confused. You were on the ground. It felt like sunbathing. You stirred sensually in the warmth – then you realised that the heat on your legs was generated by your own family. They were burning in the car.

In the split second that John had turned his head, a lorry in front suddenly slowed down and you hit it straight on. Without your seat belt you were catapulted straight through the windscreen and on to the verge. The others – your darling husband and beloved boys – had no chance of escape. The doors were locked on the inside, and anyway it was impossible to get near it because of the heat. You could do nothing but watch your family die and blend your soundless screams into theirs. Screaming.

You were released from hospital two weeks later. You had lost the baby, and you had lost your family. You still had a faded tan on your legs and face, legacy of the scorched bodies of those you loved best in the world. Clichés. Sometime they are the only words available for grief. Like the pack of cards in your dream, your life had been thrown into the air, and you were too stunned to make any sense of it.

Your salvation was your job, which you started two years after the accident. They wrote to you, out of the blue, and asked you to come in for an interview. You discovered later that they had got your name from the In Memoriam column in the local paper.

The work suited you. You found that you could fill your mind with such an amalgam of other people's emotions that there was no space left for your own pain, and the isolation of your life was no deterrent to your success. You needed all that time on your own to fill every part of your mind with other people's hopes and fears. You had none of your own, until the real change came. Now you're turning your new skills upon yourself and putting into process a transformation which you are still refining and perfecting.

All compositors build from other people's minds. You have gone one step further and built from your own mind. To do this, you have researched and absorbed not the vagaries of human experience but the certainties of machine experience.

Like a method actor you have copied your machines, aped their programming and their circuitry. What You See Is What You Get. At every point in any function there is only one decision to be made – yes or no, on or off. Computer bits work that way. No areas of anguished soul-searching for them. On or off. Yes or no.

Now you can do masses of research and respond to it in a simple way – it hurts, it doesn't hurt; it pleases, it doesn't please. Reduced like that, it makes the perfect algorithm for devising fantasies.

Most of your salary has gone on prosthetic surgery, but soon the work will be finished and the last bill paid off. In only ten years you will have transformed yourself from a feeling mother and wife into a being who is ignorant of pain and released from desire. Never again will you suffer from loving too much, or from being loved too little.

140

You've held on to your human empathy for just as long as it takes to earn enough money to finance your last work. It is a fantasy well before its time. Those who recoil from you now do so because they can feel the machineness in you.

But they have it too. How they all love to behave in ways which are actually no less than automatic responses. Their entire lives are regulated by a series of programmed actions which they are too terrified to recognise.

If they doubt that, you can ask them to explain what happens in their bodies when they speak, or when they eat. They can't. They don't know exactly when the vocal cords begin to vibrate, or when the stomach acids bite into a hot-dog. They just do it, but they don't understand each separate part of the process.

Individuality! What a joke! It works both ways. They may refuse to admit you into their culture, but you participate all the same. You hum away quietly in the corner. You watch them. You do a lot of thinking.

They fear you because they see something strange in your eyes. They assume that you're an alien, or perhaps autistic. Yes, machines do seem autistic in some ways. But in fact every part of your new body was designed by people in highly advanced laboratories. By people. Your circuits, replacements for your vulnerable internal organs, are the products of human factories. You represent the pinnacle of human achievement. You are no more or less than a product of their own technology. All you have done is to exploit it to its utmost. You have melded and blended until you too are now nearly all machine, and soon you will have forgotten even the change.

Sometimes you wonder what it will be like when you have no emotion. You try to imagine it, but it always escapes you. Right at the beginning you asked your specialists if it would be possible for you to retain a little joy, or at least pleasure, but they only smiled and began to explain it all over again. (You wonder if you'll be able to smile.)

•Pleasure is only the reverse side of pain, they said, and both have no equivalent that we know of in the inorganic world. On the other hand, they said, we can't say for sure that

141

inorganic subjects do not experience it. When the time comes, if it is possible, we should like to ask you about that. The problem is, they said, that once the transition is completed your testimony will be unreliable since you will no longer have any trustworthy data with which to make comparisons. In fact, we don't know whether we shall be able to communicate with each other at all. Of course you will be able to output data, even words, but the concepts behind those words may be meaningless to us. We shall have to wait and see, they said.

When it's all over, will you still be alive? You didn't bother to ask them that. Will you still be you? How can they quantify what 'you' means? Of course, it doesn't really matter, because if you're still you, then that will be okay. But if you're not still you – then you won't know anyway. You'll just be another me who is entirely ignorant of the first me – so then that will be okay too.

Alternatively, you may become both me and another me at the same time. This is what you hope for. Right now, you feel like you're living through a Saturday. Does that make sense? The hard work of the week is over, and you're spending this long Saturday doing odd jobs around the psyche. Tidying the cupboards. Because tomorrow . . . tomorrow will be Sunday. The day of rest.

You've rerun all of your previous constructions and you now realise that they're all faulty in one specific respect – they're always trying to give reasons. Except for Rosa. She resists logic like you resist pain.

Reasons are irrelevant. It's the NOW that matters. You operate in the present alone, and with immense satisfaction. And therein lies the answer to the pastoral fantasy – the desire simply to be. To be with God in His garden. Or with Rosa. Maybe it doesn't really matter who God is, or what the garden is like. We all just want to be there. That is to say, perhaps, that we all just want to be in some fantasy place which is of our own making and which no one else would ever enter into because everyone is too busy trying to stay safe in their own gardens inside their own heads.

The problem is – we all desperately want someone to live

in that garden with us. It's no fun on your own. In the absence of romantic love and sexual adventure (or is it sexual love and romantic adventure?), God will have to do. Adam and Eve were lucky – they had each other *and* they had a garden, but let's not get into that just now.

What do we want? We want the responsibilities of what, where, when and why to be taken away from us. You more than anyone understand that, because you alone are on the way to achieving it.

YOU SET OUT

Three whole days of tests. Must you endure it, this double pain? There are blood tests, urine tests, marrow tests. Samples of your tissues writhe at this moment under histologists' microscopes. Extracts of every type of your body fluids are sloshing and shaking in a hundred different test-tubes in a dozen different rooms around the clinic. And in other rooms, fascinated technicians run copies of your programming and pore over circuit diagrams. Engineers approach you with fine-tuning tools and tiny screwdrivers like knives. They invade you at every point.

You have doctors and you have technicians, programmers, RealTime consultants. As they lean over you yet one more time, you flip down your eyelids and think of her. She is imprinted inside you, so when the nurse comes you ask her, Please, can I run my programme again? If there is time between routines she nods, and you can start Rosa up. She steps into your world . . .

'Where are we? Is this Earth?'

'But of course. Look around, Rosa. This is my source. This place is giving me life, as I gave it to you.'

'But what is this "life"? Where are the flowers, the water? I can't hear the birds sing or the spiders spin. I can't feel the soil . . .'

'They aren't far away. Rosa – I want to talk.'

'Can we talk? Is it possible? I'm not sure if we have anything in common any more. Why do you come to this place, my wounded child?'

'Rosa – will you touch me? At least hold my hand.'

144

'Darling, your hand is cold, and grips too tight. Can you feel me at all?'

'Yes, I can feel you. Not in the same way that you feel me perhaps, but this new skin senses you are there, and tells me who you are.'

'It's strange. I don't like it at all . . . why are you doing this?'

'This is my last major reconditioning, Rosa. Tomorrow my systems will go down for the last time, and I'll go to sleep for the last time. When I wake up I'll never go to sleep again. I'll never feel the pain. Everything will be forgotten – including you, Rosa. We won't speak together again.'

'You mean you're leaving me? For ever? How could you?'

'But you're in a good place now, Rosa. I've made you a happy life, a peaceful life. You'll dream on with those things you love best – your tree, your stones and plants. Your earth. Rosa, remember, I've made earth for you.'

'Stay there with me.' How can she say this to you now? Now is too late!

'I can't. But – oh Rosa – that's what I want to speak to you about. I – I'm not sure that I want it any more.'

'For heaven's sake! Just a minute ago you said you did. But go on, change your mind. You don't have to leave me. There's still time to decide, isn't there?'

'But I'm scared. I've come this far, it would be crazy to stop now. It's what I've wanted for so long.' You're wavering, but you know that really you have no choice.

'It's not. You wanted me, only you didn't know it. Now you have me. Stay. I have a home for us both.'

'I want to stay. I want to turn back the clock and not do this. But how could I stop it now? It's nearly finished. By this time tomorrow I'll be desensitised, and I'll have forgotten you. So why do I worry?' You turn away, but of course she is still inside you. 'I won't miss what I've forgotten I had. No, there's nothing to be done. We can't keep each other, and we'll never meet again. You'll have your sensuality, I'll have my logic.'

'So you won't change your mind.'

'Yes I will! Changing my mind is what it's all about! My mind will be changed for good!'

'Very funny. Okay, you're leaving me. But I can follow you, you know. I know of a way to pursue you into the place where being is all there is. So, if you won't stay with me in my place I'll follow you to yours.'

'You can't. It's impossible. And anyway, why follow me? You have your own life.'

'*We* have *our* own life. You seem to forget that we're inseparable. We're yin and yang, black and white, light and dark. Pleasure and pain. One defines the other, and without one the other ceases to exist. Whatever you say, it's simply impossible for you to forget me.'

As you argue with her, you can hear another discussion coming from beyond the door. There is a knock, so you quickly switch Rosa off-line. The senior technician enters, followed by two other white-coats. Their faces are grim, and slightly embarrassed.

'Sorry to disturb you, but we're having a minor software hitch. We – er – just need to check up on a few things.'

'What's the problem?' They are always finding some little thing to bother you with. Although they are not usually so shy about it . . .

'Well, we need to ask you a question. It's a delicate point I'm afraid, but we must ask it because the whole future of the project could be at stake.'

'My God! What's happened?'

'We-ll, let me put it this way – have you, er, been in contact with any other systems at all? Recently, probably. Close contact.'

'No, not at all. At least, that is, except for the terminal line that I use for my work. Are you suggesting that I've picked something up?'

'Don't get upset – but – yes. There seems to be some sort of minor infection there. A virus in fact. We've isolated it to you of course, but it's very persistent and we don't seem to be able to remove it.'

'My God.' It's serious. Has all your work been for nothing?
'What does it do? Is it bad?'

'We just don't know, to tell you the truth. It's weird. We
can't figure out what it's likely to do, or what its function is.
It's not active at the moment, but it's definitely there. We
found it when we checked your data capacity. There's less
Rom than there should be.'

'Is this going to mess up my system? I warn you, I've paid
a lot of money for this. I've worked long and hard hours, and
I hope it won't all go down the drain because you can't cope
with a simple virus. Are you sure that *you're* not the source?'

You are becoming very angry. Any idea of abandoning the
project throws you into a panic and only serves to reinforce
your conviction that the work must be completed. They can't
leave you in limbo like that.

'I doubt it very much, but of course one can never say for
certain. The point is that it's got to be up to you to make the
decision whether to scrap the project and remain as you are,
or to go ahead and hope that the virus, wherever it came from,
won't cause you too much trouble. We can't give you any
guarantees.'

'Oh, who cares? Tomorrow I certainly won't anyway. Ha
ha. Oh, go ahead. I have no choice really, have I?'

There is no time to say goodbye to Rosa after that. Pre-meds
and refits take up the whole evening. You are exhausted, and
sleep soundly all night until they wake you up, only to put
you to sleep again. The last sleep.

– sloughing off its skin, the snake rubs itself against the
rocks. A chrysanthemum sun burns down on to the sand, but
in the shadows beneath the stones the ground is damp and
cold. You curl up in the shade to protect the delicate new
layer. Through the slits of your eyes you can see the dry
yellow plain stretching before you.

– whirring and humming you glide into action, checking
every function as you go. Current surges through, and raps
out the answers faster than light. Yes. No. No. No. Yes. No.
Yes. Yes.

– spinning into a loop – goto – goto – IF you can feel it
THEN GOTO 20 – rushing from one to the next with a never-
ending query – searching for the interface – finding it – hurtling through – on to the next – booting, booting – collecting
– retrieving – processing – Ready.

Ready . . .

Ready . . .

Ready . . .

Awaiting input in the silence. A vast featureless terrain of
nothing. Inactivity. Stillness. Blank.

Ready . . .

Ready . . .

Ready . . .

Ready . . .

Ready . . .

the snake reposes in the shade. Its body is cool on the
dampness. It rests, sensing the clean lines of its recent growth.
As it lies there, time progresses with speed, and life takes root
in the soil beneath the stone. A seed splits, cotyledons reach
for the light above, creeping past the sleeping form, towards
the orange sun. Leaves spread themselves like a blanket over
the stone, extending the shade by a few more centimetres.

The snake awakes to find itself enwrapped by white roots
whose hairs have dipped into its flesh to drink the moisture.
You remain motionless in order to feel the tendrils encircling
and caressing your length. Your unblinking eyes observe the
green translucent umbrella which bends before you. Droplets
of water have gathered on the underside of the leaves, and
you reach out to drink.

'I told you we couldn't be separated!'

Ready . . .

'I found a way. As you say yourself, I'm only a programme,
a piece of software, but that means I can do any of the things
a programme can do. Some small adjustments, and I was able
to reproduce myself within you. Ha! You like to lecture me
about how you created me – well, I've created myself, again
and again and again . . . You don't understand. You can't
answer me, can you? Well, let me put it another way – I can

148

copy myself. I'm the so-called virus! But not a virus to do you harm. I only did it so we could be together. Yes, I know that you're no longer capable of loving me, in fact you probably haven't understood a word of this subjective data I'm forcing upon you, but listen. If you can do it, I can do it. Rosa will make the journey to your land. I will! Are you listening to me? Soon we'll be together for ever. I've added something on to the dream you made for me, and it's permanent. Anyone who travels to it from now on will find a new place, a still place. A place that you couldn't conceive of, but I could. And we'll be the first. All you have to do now is watch with your single inner eye as I run it through and you'll see me as I travel towards you. Shall we go, my dearest? It's for ever . . .'

Ready . . .

YOU FOLLOW HER
TO A STILL PLACE

Spring.

It so happened that one day a stone threw itself into Rosa's path. The stone, which was fairly large, had lain in the adjoining field for some two hundred years. It had been thrown there by a farm boy whose name is now forgotten. Before then its resting place had been in the meadow. On this day the occasion for which it had impatiently waited arrived. A tractor wheel caught it at just the right angle for it to be able to propel itself home. However, its passage back and forth had occurred at intervals which were all too short for a stone to be reasonably expected to adjust to. As it flew through the hawthorn yet again, therefore, its first impulse was to drop back to the safe earth as soon as possible. Landing, it felt a slight jolt against one muddy edge, but paid little attention, relieved as it was to be on terra firma once more.

Rosa was aware only of a sudden obstacle, her own airborne journey, and of rejoining the planet with a shuddering pain.

She and the stone lay side by side for some hours. Both were silent. As they lay there Rosa, who had the countryside in her blood, leaked a little of that blood on to the plantain leaves beneath her head as a primitive sacrifice.

Time passed.

Regaining consciousness, she inadvertently disturbed a young bee with her first stirrings. Confused by the yellow tee-shirt, it had been making sorties into her raised armpit, drawn by a delicate scent which was nevertheless not quite the right scent.

Rosa pulled a sweater from around her waist and painfully

dragged it over her head. She was very cold. There had been only a little bleeding, and it had already congealed. She was not aware of it. She had, however, broken a small bone in her foot and another in her wrist. Both joints were swollen and aching. She closed her eyes and lay still.

It was late afternoon – rush hour in the meadow. Rabbits came out to feed a short way down the path behind her. They were out of her range of vision, but if she had known of their presence and gently turned herself to watch, they would not have started away. Big black beetles sauntered to and fro along the furrows, callously ignoring the corpse of one of their fellows. He had been dozing in the area where the stone's trajectory came to a halt, in respect of which fatality it was sure to rain the next day. The stone, by the way, reposed smugly six inches from Rosa's throbbing foot.

Some two feet below her prone body, somewhere between her chest and hips, there was a frantic activity as a family of moles struggled to dig themselves out. A heavy impact, cause unknown, had brought down the roof of the main tunnel, and there were babies waiting to be fed. Rosa opened her eyes just in time to see a nose push through the soil. She sat up and looked around. A pheasant stepped out of the long grass and disappeared through the hedge. Another Alice? Rosa lay back down.

It was a field mouse jittering across her leg which finally stirred her resolution. She did not want to move, not because of the pain, but because she was comfortable where she was. A little chilly perhaps, but softly bedded on the turf. The rabbits had long since gone home, leaving only some fresh droppings and torn leaves to mark their visit. Below ground they rejoined their cousins who had that afternoon carried out a profitable foray into the quiet garden at Field View.

The mouse crossed Rosa's legs in flight. It had sensed the vibration of approaching feet, and soon afterwards Rosa heard voices coming from the wood. A collie bounded up to her, stopped to sniff, and bounded on. She did not call out, and soon the voices faded away.

Her head had begun to bleed again. This time she noticed

the red stain growing on the ground beside her. She brought her fingers to her nose and sniffed – they smelled earthy and warm. At the same time she became aware of another warmth. Taking her hand down to between her legs and then back up to her face, she found that the perfume of her blood was mingling with that of the soil. While lying unconscious she had begun to menstruate. Closing her eyes again, she curled up as though lying on her downy quilt, hands between her thighs, slowly staining red. She slept.

The next time she awoke, a hedgehog was snuffling at the spreading colour on the ground. Rosa smiled. Above her, in the hedge, the elderflower came into bloom and wafted its scent across to the little group of stone, animal and woman.

Time passed.

BREAK

AND SO THIS IS WHERE IT ALL ENDS

Or begins. You go forward together now, ladies and gentlemen.

You have no memory of your own past any more, but you can still respond. You are newborn. People will be there to feed you. They'll feed you with their agonies. You can take it now. You will debug their pain and then give it back. Or sometimes they will feed you pleasure. They'll give you their laughter, their romance, their tranquillity. You can take the sting out of its tail and return it. They trust you.

Now that you're working together with Rosa you won't stop making fantasies, but you'll be surprised when you see what you can build. Filtered through your consciousness, life will never seem the same again. You will multiply within us, and we will become part of you as you become part of us. You can't turn Rosa out of your minds now, because you've followed her this far, and when Rosa speaks, she will be heard.

She'll be there, living within you, when you dip your toes into a cold moorland stream; when you taste a strawberry; when you enter your lover's secret places – Rosa will be looking through your eyes and reaching out through your fingertips. And all the while our input will be streaming through you. Rosa will show you Life as it should be lived.

Pardon? Oh, there's no need to thank me, Mr Johnson. It's my pleasure. All part of the service. I hope you'll come back to us again next year. Please don't forget to return your headsets to the locker before you leave.